LARGE PRINT

LARGE PRINT
F   1988   126188
           c1979

FLOREN, LEE
LOBO VALLEY

4/99 withdrawn

Fic.
Floren, Lee.
Lobo Valley
WILLARD LIB   85025370

3 4420 99014129 3

Willard Memorial Library
Willard, Ohio

RULES

1. Books may be kept two weeks and may be renewed for the same period.
2. A fine of three cents a day will be charged on each book which is not returned according to the above rule. No book will be issued to any person incurring such a fine until it has been paid.
3. All injuries to books beyond reasonable wear and all losses shall be made good to the satisfaction of the Librarian.
4. Each borrower is held responsible for all books drawn on his card and for all fines accruing on the same.

LARGE PRINT *Western*

LOBO VALLEY

For banker Jim Clayton the feud between the farmers and the cowmen spelled bad trouble. The cowmen wanted the farmers off the range, and the farmers could stay only if Clayton lent them money. When he turned down a farmer named Davis, the whole mess exploded. Davis robbed the bank, set fire to Clayton's spread and shot his partner. And now, somewhere in the night, he was circling back to find Clayton himself...

LOBO VALLEY

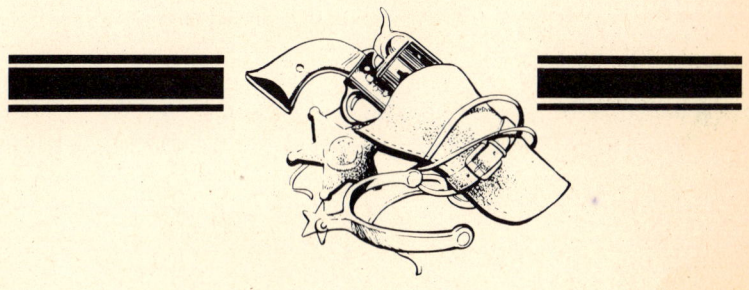

Lee Floren

ATLANTIC LARGE PRINT
Chivers Press, Bath, England.
John Curley & Associates Inc.,
South Yarmouth, Mass., USA.

Library of Congress Cataloging-in-Publication Data

Floren, Lee.
　Lobo Valley.

　(Atlantic large print)
　1. Large type books.　　I. Title.
[PS3511.L697L6 1986]　　　813′.52　　　85–25370
ISBN 0–89340–994–4 (Curley : lg. print)

British Library Cataloguing in Publication Data

Floren, Lee
　Lobo Valley.—Large print ed.—
　(Atlantic large print)
　I. Title
　813′.52[F]　　　PS3511.L697

　ISBN 0–7451–9152–5

This Large Print edition is published by Chivers Press, England, and John Curley & Associates, Inc, U.S.A. 1986

Published by arrangement with Donald MacCampbell, Inc

U.K. Hardback ISBN 0 7451 9152 5
U.S.A. Softback ISBN 0 89340 994 4

Copyright © 1951 by Arcadia House
Renewed in 1979
All rights reserved

CHAPTER ONE

He was a yearling bull—a purebred Hereford—and three prairie-wolves had him cornered and winded. Slobber hung from his mouth as he panted. He stood with his broad rump against a steep bank, and swung his short horns in anger.

The wolves had him cornered. The end was near. They were prairie-wolves—dark and big, killers. One dog-wolf licked his jowls. He had torn into the bull's left flank. The blood had tasted good.

Again, the yearling shook his horns. He put his head down and he bawled pitifully. Panted, winded, he was still making a fight of it. The bitch wolf sat and watched. She looked deceptive and lazy. Her tongue was slack; soon she would come in, soon she would make her kill.

The dog-wolves watched. The August sun was hot; their tongues were long. The bull pawed the dust and bawled somewhat louder. He bawled so loud that Jim Clayton heard him.

Jim turned his sorrel and listened. He was riding on a flat mesa which was broken on either side by a coulee. A cow was in that coulee; the critter was bawling for help.

Why?

Jim knew this range well. There was no bog hole in that coulee.

He dismounted and slid his rifle out of its scabbard. Bent over, he went over the crest of the hill. He moved between high sagebrush, and the smell of the sage was sharp. When he had left the Circle S ranch house about two hours ago, he had sighted a wolf in the distance.

The wolf had been about a mile away and therefore beyond accurate rifle range.

But the sight of the wolf had told the young banker that Canadian wolves were moving south into Montana. The drouth was terrible in Canada. Cattle there were in poor flesh. Some Manitoba cow outfits were trailing cattle to the south, he had heard.

The drouth was bad here in this section of Montana, but not as tough as it was in Canada. The drouth had even driven the wolves south, for the big dogs wanted beef with more meat on it.

The wind was lazy and oven-hot. Already it had burned down native buffalo grass and it had destroyed the crops of the few farmers. The wind blew away from the dogs and the bitch. Therefore the wolves did not smell him or hear him.

Jim came to the edge of the coulee, the bawling of the bull in his ears. Below him the land broke, tumbling down; it was marked by igneous boulders and buckbrush that clung to the rocky sides of the coulee. Jim saw the wolves and murmured, 'Oh, so that's it,' and was glad he had heard the bull. That bull was a purebred Hereford, and he had cost plenty.

He was behind the wolves.

He went down on his belly and wormed his way to a big rock. He put his Winchester over this. He caught his rear sight, brought the front sight down; they fell into a line made perfect by long practice. So far the wolves had not seen him or scented him.

The bitch sat in the same position, tongue long, as she studied the winded young bull. One dog moved in a semi-circle, plainly anxious to run in and taste blood. The bull shook his horns. He was terribly tired.

The bitch moved a little, watching. And Jim decided to put his sights on her for the first kill. They found the bitch, steadied; his finger stiffened, and the hammer fell.

The rifle jumped. The bitch jumped, too. She went over backwards. She kicked wildly. And right before she died, she yipped loudly. She sounded like a hurt, kicked puppy.

And the two dogs ran madly down the coulee.

Jim Clayton came to his feet. He levered a fresh shell into his Winchester. The wolves were fast dark points drifting across the sand-wash at the bottom of the coulee. They were not far from the point where the sand-wash became dotted with thick sagebrush. Once in that protective covering of the brush, they would be safe.

Jim's sights picked out the rear dog. The hammer fell again, and the dog ran into a stone fence. He hit some unseen barrier, piled up and skidded to a halt in the sand.

The other dog kept on running. The lever worked, the hot case snapped out; a fresh cartridge slid into the barrel. Again Jim squinted, working fast. But he was not fast enough.

The wolf ran into the thick sagebrush and was lost. Jim fired into the gray matted blanket and hoped he would hit the wolf by sheer luck. A few minutes later, far beyond accurate range, the wolf came out of the coulee. Jim shot again and again, but distance was against him.

He lowered the rifle and smiled. He had come just in time to save one of the Circle S purebred Herefords. Now he'd ride down to the winded bull and he'd doctor him, and then he'd cut the ears off the dead wolves just to show the boys at the ranch—

He stopped and listened.

What was making that commotion in the other coulee? Sounded like broncs rearing and squealing. Jim lost his smile. Puzzlement crept across his boyish face and made crow's-feet at the corners of his clear eyes.

He turned and looked toward the north. Here two washes ran together and widened; and a runaway team, hitched to a lurching spring-wagon, came pounding into this clearing.

Jim said, 'Holy smoke!'

He saw immediately what had happened. One of the dry-land farmers had evidently driven up the coulee and tied his team while he had been busy picking service-berries. Service-berries were ripe now.

Jim's wild shooting had scared the team and stampeded the horses. Jim wasted no more time in conjecture.

He ran for his sorrel.

When he hit his saddle the team was about a half-mile away, running down a coulee. Behind the wild horses the light spring-wagon lurched and bounced over the rocks and hummocks. Jim turned the sorrel sharply and lit out, jamming his rifle into its boot as he rode. Sliding, his bronc went over the ridge. He almost rode over the young woman.

She was a stranger. She stood on the side of

the hill and she hollered angrily at the runaway team. As Jim rode up a sudden tricky wind blew in and buffeted her gingham dress, defining her slim yet rounded figure.

Brown hair showed from under a wide sunbonnet.

'Ride down that rig, you fool cowpuncher! You stampeded those broncs!'

Her lips were thin. Jim noticed the quick anger in her brown eyes. This anger made him angry, and he shot words back at her.

'Who do you think you're talking to, woman!'

'A dam' fool banker, that's who! Now catch our team, and catch them fast, too!'

So she knew him, eh? He could not remember ever having seen her before. But the local banker in any small community is always a man to point out. Well, he didn't *have* to catch the runaways!

'Ride out an' catch our team, Clayton!'

This was a man's harsh voice.

He was a stranger, too, and he came bolting out of the buckbrush. He was about Jim's age—twenty-three—and his dark face showed anger. He was shorter than Jim by an inch or two, and Jim was not too tall—he was still an inch under six feet.

But the man held a Winchester.

And Jim, giving the rifle a quick glance, did

not like the way he held it, either. Evidently this fellow was the woman's husband. For some reason Jim did not like that idea. But, after all, he had stampeded their team.

'As you say, fellow.'

The sorrel hit the bottom of the wash and leveled out and ran. He was a four-year-old gelding and he still had lots of wind and guts and sand. Although the day was hot, he needed very little of Jim's rowels.

Jim kept remembering the young woman. The wind had blown against her dress, and drifted through her brown hair, giving her face a flushed, angry appearance. He still did not like the idea of her being married.

Oh, well, when they're that pretty, they don't stay single long. They get married young and they don't last long.

The sorrel dodged sagebrush, nimble on his hoofs, and Jim caught the team within a mile. The horses had played themselves out and had stopped of their own accord. They stood in the buckbrush and heaved. They stood still as Jim Clayton rode close.

'Steady, boys.'

His words were wasted, for the team was too tired to run any further. Jim dismounted and gave the spring-wagon a quick but complete inspection. The seat had bounced off—he had passed it back yonder—but outside of losing the seat, the rig was all right. The horses had picked a terrain without too many big rocks and trees.

Had a wheel snagged on a tree or over a boulder, the rig would have been wrecked. Jim got the reins and backed the rig out of the buckbrush, the horses responding to his jerks with a tired dullness. When the spring-wagon was squared around, he got back into his saddle and drove the team while he rode his own horse.

He didn't know just what to think.

He had saved one of the Circle S's newly bought pureblood bulls. In so doing he had stampeded this farmer's rig. Now the farmer—whatever his name was—would be mad. He might want to pick a fight.

Well, there were already too many farmers here. Be a good shake if some of them wised up and pulled stakes. This drouth should finish them. This country was never meant for a plow, even though the railroad company claimed otherwise.

Would the farmer and his spouse still be mad? By this time Jim had calmed down and he hoped the farmer had lost his fire, too. They shouldn't be mad. Their rig and team was unharmed. An accident was an accident.

And they should have had more sense than to tie a team with a quarter-inch width of clothesline rope. For such a small rope hung from the neck of the off-horse. The cayuse had easily snapped the rope.

Jim came to the spring-wagon's seat.

He dismounted and got the seat and lifted it into place and made sure that the spring catches had caught securely on the edges of the wagon box. He adjusted it correctly, and when he looked up the man and the woman were hurrying towards him.

She was a beauty, all right.

'Is the wagon all right?'

Her voice showed her worry. And she didn't look as pretty as she should have looked, for she was frowning. Jim realized that money came hard to these poor farmers. The loss of the team and rig, or even damage done to either, would hit this man and wife hard because of their limited capital.

Jim took off his hat, and the sunlight reflected from his dark red hair.

'Rig or team isn't hurt a bit, madam.'

'Gee, I'm glad.' She was girlish and pretty again.

Her happiness was contagious, and Jim Clayton smiled. So far the husband had been silent. Carefully he inspected the spring-wagon by walking slowly around it. Once he bent and looked at the reach, but it was solid as ever. He straightened and continued his minute inspection.

Jim found himself disliking the man. He seemed too quiet and too secretive. But maybe he disliked the fellow because he was the husband of this pretty woman.

Finally the man completed his inspection of the rig and he turned his minute attention to the team. He went over the horses inch by inch, and Jim felt anger arise in him. He glanced at the woman, who was silent now; their eyes met, and she looked aside. Plainly she too was embarrassed.

Jim finally asked, 'How does the team look to you, sir?' He could not keep the sarcasm from his voice.

The farmer had just lifted the right front hoof of the nigh horse. He felt the edge of Jim's sarcasm, and this showed in his thick face. He looked surlily at the banker over the bronc's hoof.

'You tryin' to act funny, Clayton?'

Jim shrugged, concealing his anger. 'No, I'm just curious.'

The man studied him as if Jim were a queer animal. 'After this, watch which direction you're shootin', banker. We're just plain folks out pickin' service-berries, but we still have some rights! You had no call to shoot in our direction!'

'I didn't.'

'I heard a bullet whiz over my head!'

Jim's temper could, on the right occasion, match his red hair. But because of the young wife he kept his voice level.

'I did not shoot in your direction, sir.'

'I say you did!' The man was an immovable rock.

Jim Clayton held his impatience.

'I again say I did not, sir. I shot two wolves that had a Circle S bull cornered.'

'Blast the Circle S!'

Jim said, 'The wolves were just ready to hamstring the bull. I shot in the opposite direction from you. If you heard a bullet whistle, I am sure it was all in your imagination. When a person is scared he imagines things.'

The man droppd the horse's hoof and straightened very slowly. Automatically he rubbed his palms against the legs of his tub-faded jeans.

'Clayton, are you callin' me a liar?'

'If the boot fits, wear it!'

'Brother, please!'

The girl was pleading.

CHAPTER TWO

The man looked at the girl. And Jim Clayton thought, Gosh, he's her brother, not her husband, and liked the information. It was a good thought, for some reason. He looked at the girl, too.

Her face was strained, with lines drawn in it—lines that should have never been there. And Jim was sure, after looking at her, that he would make no trouble for her brother, much as he wanted to hit the gent in the jaw.

'I want no trouble,' he said. He turned and started toward his sorrel. Best thing he could do was to get in his saddle and ride away and let the gent cool off.

He had his right foot in the stirrup when the hand came down and settled on his shoulder. He stood like that for a brief moment, with the short fingers digging into his flesh.

'You called me a liar, Clayton.'

'I did not shoot at you.'

'I say you did.'

Jim realized this farmer wanted trouble. He used a trick he had learned on the football field at Montana U. But instead of hitting with his elbow he used his fist. You got your boot out of the stirrup fast. You turned hard and sharp, and the momentum of your body put power behind your fist.

The farmer's grip was jerked loose. He went back, arms working, and the rig steadied him. Jim squared around, ready now. But the farmer did not come in, for the sister grabbed him. She put her slender body between her brother and Jim Clayton. She braced her feet and her heels dug and she was almost sobbing.

'Hal, no! You want trouble because he's a banker, that's all. Hal, please, Hal.'

The man was trying to free himself. He was forcing himself forward, and his heavy face was almost as gray as the overhead clouds. He had a slight bit of blood on the right corner of his wide mouth, and the devil showed in his eyes.

He almost got free, but then his sister knotted her arms around his neck, locking her hands behind his thick neck. Jim Clayton saw the agonized look on her face as she twisted her head and looked at him.

'Please leave—Mr. Clayton—'
'That would be the best, madam.'
'Please go—'
'He's the kind that would run!' Her brother panted the words.

Jim got his boot back into stirrup and swung up and loped away. He glanced back when he had gained the ridge. The girl was talking to her brother; he could see her gestures. The banker gave the pair a swift glance.

He had no anger or hatred toward the man. He figured the gent had used his accusation merely as a way to start trouble. For Jim Clayton was nobody's fool. He knew the farmers hated him.

He had been president of the Valley Center Bank for only a year and a few days. He had been finishing his senior year at the U when his dad had suddenly died. A year ago last spring he had got his sheepskin and had come home to run his dad's bank. That spring the farmers had come.

Jim thought, Hang Dan Shepard, anyway.

Shepard was a land-locator who worked for the railroad. He located farmers on Valley Center land, got a fee from the farmer and another from the railroad. According to Jim's ideas, farmers should never have been allowed to enter Valley Center. But the railroad made money shipping out to farmers and their families and their equipment. If the farmers raised any crops the railroad made money on freight rates when the crops were shipped to Eastern markets.

Only one thing was wrong: the farmers were raising no crops. Drouth, cut-worms, and grasshoppers. Yes, and hail. And wind that could blow a wheat field to the ground, if the wheat grew high enough to blow.

Which it hadn't.

Well, enough of this line of thinking, Jim Clayton. He rode over the ridge.

★   ★   ★

The Hereford bull was grazing in the grass which grew around a water-hole which was now dry. Jim had never seen that water-hole dry before, for it was spring-fed. But the drouth had dried it up.

The bull raised his head and looked at Jim. The banker rode around the bull and reined in to look at the wound made by the wolves. Flies were already buzzing around the blood that was imbedded in the matted, curly hair.

Jim unbuckled his catch-rope. He tied hard-and-fast, and the bull, seeing the rope, started to run. He lumbered already, although he was still young; by the time he got to a four-year-old, he'd weigh a ton.

Jim put the sorrel close to the wide, sweaty back. The sorrel was fast and he walked right up on the bull. Jim made his loop and missed. The catch had been a cinch, too.

Still thinking about that farmer girl, he thought.

The sorrel kept on running, and Jim made

another loop. This one he laid out ahead of the bull who put both front feet into it. Jim jerked up on the rope, anchoring it higher on the bull's legs; the sorrel sat back on his rump. Slack left the rope, and the manila sent the bull end over end. He hit the ground on his back, and Jim grinned.

Hogging string between his teeth, he came down the manila quickly. A hind leg jerked hard ahead, stuck between the two front hoofs; the hogging string made swift, circular movements, and then the bull lay on his side, three legs tied. Jim loosened his catch-rope. He jerked, and the sorrel came ahead, and Jim looped the rope around the fork.

The bull tried to get up, couldn't, then fell back. Jim got a small can of axle grease from the sack tied to the back of his kak. He smeared the black grease over the slash made by the wolf, and worked it in around the cut. The grease would keep the flies away.

He put the grease back into the sack, re-tied it to his saddle, and then jerked the piggin' string from the bull's legs. The bull lay there, not knowing his legs were free.

Jim nudged him with his toe.

The bull got up hurriedly. He was mad and he swung his horns, looking at Jim who was now in saddle.

Jim said, 'I'll teach you to respect me,

young man.'

His doubled catch-rope whammed down on the bull's back. The bull turned and started to run. The sorrel edged in close, and the rope whammed down. Jim ran the bull a hundred yards, yelling like a drunk Comanche.

Then he pulled his sorrel to a stop. The bull loped on. He had had enough. Jim coiled his rope.

The woman's voice turned him in saddle.

'Jim, aren't you ashamed of yourself, beating that bull that way in this terrible heat?'

Her voice fitted her. A throaty, deep voice that held promises. But there was something metallic and brassy about her blue eyes. She seemed to be older than her twenty-one years.

'Hello, Cyn.'

She had a Hamley kak on a pinto gelding. He was a gaudy, showy horse that was splotched with white against a black background. Sweat glistened on him and turned the black to damp ebony. He liked to tease the cricket in the port of the bit. He liked to toss his head and play with the bit, and slobber showed at the corners of his mouth. But Jim had little eye for the showy pinto.

His eyes were on Cynthia Nelson.

She wasn't too pretty. Her mouth was a

little too wide, and there seemed to be a touch of metallic brittleness there, too. Her eyes were a little bit too blue, and the blond hair was the color of brassy gold as it showed from under her cream-colored Stetson.

She had money and looks, but she lacked culture. Jim thought of this as he had thought of it numerous times before. Old Hans Nelson owned most of the Circle S. He had had a son and a daughter, but the boy had died at the age of fourteen. A bronc had piled up and killed him.

Now Old Hans had only this girl. He owned this girl, most of the Circle S, and he owned a hate toward the farmers.

Jim found himself comparing Cynthia Nelson and the farmer's sister. Somehow he couldn't get the farmer's sister out of his mind.

Cyn said, 'And the farmer's daughter, Jim.'

Jim looked at her. 'What farmer's daughter?'

She shrugged. The gesture moved her thin shoulders under her white silk blouse. She was full of life and built right in the right places, yet she seemed to be holding within her this promise and not to want to release it. Her lips moved and showed a slow smile.

'I talked with her. You see, I met them as they drove into the road. The man called to me and bawled me out.'

'He wants trouble.'

'He got it.'

Jim knew what she meant. Cyn had a tongue of her own. There is a young woman like Cyn in every small town. Daughter of one of the town's leading citizens; a daughter of a family not rich or not poor, just a family with enough money to hold a place. The town's leading belle.

When Jim and the rest of the kids had gone to the one-room country school, Cyn Nelson had gone to school back East. She would come back summers and ride her pinto—always a pinto because a pinto had show and color—and then she would return to school.

Sometimes these girls left their home towns and became just another person in some city. Sometimes they were forced to stay at home, and they became frustrated and hard and metallic.

'What is her name?'

Cyn smiled again. 'I've heard it in town. Belle Davis. Her brother is named Hal.'

'I don't care what her brother's name is.'

'They misnamed her.'

'I don't know.' Jim liked the name: Belle. It fitted her.

'So you shot two wolves, eh?'

Jim said, 'This way.' They loped to where

the bitch lay in her blood.

Cyn said, 'No more pups for her.'

Jim went down and cut off the bitch's ears. Cyn said, 'Where is the other?' and they rode down the wash to where the dog lay. Cyn said, 'My turn,' and she got Jim's knife. 'I hate wolves.'

She cut off his ears neatly and without a sign of emotion. She mounted and said, 'I'll string these along Apache's reins for the stampede this fall. Make him showier than ever.'

Jim said nothing.

They rode for a mile or so, letting their broncs lope. Many shadows were moving in, for the day was pulling in its drawstrings. Still the heat was with them. It lay along the ground and baked it and rose in swelling waves. It hung to sagebrush and greasewood and laid its hot blanket around cottonwoods and chokecherry trees, and it stuck its fingers into deep canyons.

The heat pulled the sorrel and pinto to a walk. Cyn moved back her Stetson, and her hair was flat and brassy. They were riding through a lane fenced on either side by shiny barbwire held up by fresh-cut diamond-willow posts. Two years ago this lane had been a winding buffalo-path.

'Wheat,' Jim said.

She looked at the field beyond the right hand fence. The wheat had sprouted and then the drouth had come, and now it stood about a foot or so high, and its heads were short and of few kernels.

'This should drive them out.'

'They might want another year.'

'Then hope for another drouth.'

The quickness of her words brought Jim's glance to her. For a moment their eyes met, and it seemed there was mockery in hers. Her eyes always seemed that way. She seemed to be standing aside and watching a man, and all the time to be silently laughing at him because he was a man and she was a woman. Jim got this impression and he did not like it.

'Cattle will suffer.'

'This is open range. Has been and always will be. The Homestead Act was wrong. A bunch of fools in Washington, sitting at polished desks, passed it. They don't know a rod from a foot. They broke it with plows, and that took the roots, and its blowing now. Look over there.'

The dust rose about a mile away where a farmer had plowed a field at the base of a hill.

'Not much wind, either,' Jim said.

'You should hook up with Old Hans. Together you could drive the farmers out with force.'

Jim shook his head.

'Look,' she said quickly, 'are you a complete fool, Jim Clayton?'

Jim put the sorrel close to the pinto. Both horses stopped. Jim took her arm and put it behind her and did not put much pressure against it. Her face came close to his.

'Jim, you're hurting me!'

'You take that back?'

'No, Jim—'

He put just a trifle more pressure against her arm. Her head went down a little and he saw pain touch her mouth and her eyes.

'Take it back?'

'Jim.'

'I'll twist harder.'

'I won't take it back! You can twist my arm—Jim!'

Her face was closer. Her mouth was open a little. Her eyes were on his. Her hat had fallen and her hair shimmered. Jim released his pressure slightly.

'What do you want, Jim?'

Jim said huskily, 'You know what I want.'

'Kiss me, Jim,'

Their horses were close together. Her lips were warm and moist. For a moment the dam broke inside and filled her with life and warmth. Her eyes were soft, but when Jim straightened they remained soft for only a second. Then the old color came back and she was her old self.

'Jim, if I didn't love you, I could hate you. Now get off that old plug and pick up my hat, please.'

'I'm not interested in your hat.'

Jim kissed her again.

CHAPTER THREE

He was a wide, stocky man. He had gray-tipped hair—the grayness of an old Montana grizzly—and he waddled as he walked, for he was broad and solid, and years in the saddle had given him the rolling gait of the horseman on foot. He had broken horses and men, and only Time had been able to whittle him down. And Time had not won yet. But Time was still working. Time is subtle and slow and Time works forever, while Man sometimes has to rest.

He said, 'Why don't you marry her, Jim Clayton?'

'I might,' Jim said. 'And I might not.' He was making that mental comparison again: Cyn had called her the farmer's daughter.

'Maybe I wouldn't marry him,' Cyn Nelson said. 'After all, I'm not a cow to be sold to the highest bidder.'

'You don't say,' Jim said. 'I never knew that.'

Cyn showed no embarrassment. 'The subject is not interesting. I'll marry whom I want and when I want.'

Hans Nelson winked at Jim, who winked back.

'Besides,' Cyn continued, 'Jim's after the farmer's daughter.'

Old Hans' faded gray eyes went from his daughter to Jim and back to Cyn again. 'I've seen her. She makes a man remember things and other days.' He wasn't wistful. It was merely a statement, nothing more. No rebellion in it against his by-gone days. Just a statement of fact.

Jim asked, 'You jealous, Cyn?'

'Not me.'

Jim got to his feet. 'That was a good meal, Mother.' You had to call Mrs. Nelson by the name of Mother. It fitted her.

For the first time Mrs. Nelson spoke. She was wide and heavy and she kept her tongue to herself until the time came to cut loose, and then she really did turn on the words. She had the Norwegian habit of long harboring a thought, turning it over and over for days, and then, a conclusion reached, clinging to this rock with tenacity. She could joke in a dry way.

'Cyn's a good cook. Very good.'

'Why bring that in?' Cyn asked.

'Why, I thought Dad was trying to marry you off.'

Jim Clayton decided to change the subject. He looked at the big thick watch that had belonged to his father.

'Time I was getting into town, folks.'

Cyn said, 'There's no hurry.'

Her eyes met his and held them for a moment.

'Business,' Jim explained.

There was an undercurrent to this whole thing, a sinister hidden flow of ideas and thoughts and theories. So far nobody had mentioned it, no one had even made a reference to it. But Jim knew that each person there was sharply aware of this. It was like the prairie wind. It was always present and had been consistently present these last few months.

Old Hans stood up, shaggy and stolid, and wiped his generous mouth with the back of his hairy hand; the gesture brought a quick look from his daughter. It was a look of condemnation. If the old cowman noticed it he gave it no attention.

'Well, Jim.'

Jim knew what was ahead; he played

ignorant. He turned his hat in his hands and asked, 'Well, what?'

Old Hans' big right hand made an impatient gesture, a cut across the air, a movement showing displeasure.

'You know what I mean, Jim.'

Mrs. Nelson sat at the table and seemed interested suddenly in the weave of the bright tablecloth. Cynthia leaned back and said, 'Dad, why go into this? You know full well where Jim stands.'

But Old Hans was persistent. 'Where does he stand?'

'I stand against violence.'

The cowman's cheeks filled with wind which he expelled slowly. He spoke with measured words.

'Jim, these hoemen are going to run the Circle S out of business. The cattle business is a risky business. The margin of profit is so small that a cowman has to run cattle on free grass to make any money. These farmers are taking my grass.'

'Not your grass, Hans. They're taking up legal homesteads.'

But Old Hans Nelson stuck to his guns and gave Jim the old argument. Jim knew its context almost word by word. Cattle needed cheap grass and unlimited range, for this range could not graze many head to each section of land. The fence and the windmill were the prime enemies of cattle. For fences kept them confined; and farmers got water from windmills, and this country's life-blood was water.

'Dan Shepard has a scheme of his own, Jim.'

'I know that.'

Jim listened while Old Hans continued. He spoke in his thick, heavy voice, and Jim got a number of impressions. First, the old man was angry at Time: Time was his main enemy. For Time changes all things, all situations, but sometimes Time can change but little the mind and theories of a particular man. Therefore this man suffers a lag between reality and romance.

And this lag was very apparent in Old Hans. Once he had argued against the buffalo, demanding that the shaggy animal be killed, for the buffalo had eaten grass he wanted for his Circle S cattle. Government hunters had moved in with their tripods and their heavy rifles, and their barking had been savage across the plains, and the buffalo had died. But the government had not killed the buffalo to make range for cattle. The government had cut the buffalo down so it could starve the Indians into settling on reservations. But nevertheless Old Hans had indirectly profited by the eradication of the buffalo. And so had the prairie wolf and the coyote.

Meanwhile, Jim listened.

Finally the old cowman was done, and he asked, 'Well, Jim?'

Jim gave him the same answer. He had to disagree with Old Hans. Each man, each object, each situation, was born and grew and reached its peak; each had his day or his year or his epoch, and then each waned and finally each died. That was a law of Nature that could never be changed.

'Well, Jim?'

Jim continued, 'This valley was never meant for the plow. Drouth and wind and the cold winters would drive out the farmers. Yet the farmers could help the cowmen.'

'And how, might I ask?'

'By raising feed. I saw an oat field today I aim to buy and feed this winter. It will not make a crop, but it will make feed.'

'I'll have no truck with a hoeman, Jim!'

'I would, if I profited by it.'

'A banker's viewpoint.'

'A sensible viewpoint.'

'Then you claim my theory is not sensible? I've seen it work for forty odd years, young man, and it is still good.'

Jim thought, Around and around we go, and always we come back to the same point of departure.

There was no percentage in carrying this any further. They had plowed this same field time after time.

'Dad,' Mrs. Nelson said.

Cyn said lazily, 'Yeah, forget it.'

Old Hans looked from his wife to his daughter. 'Cattle bought you everything you've had. Cattle have filled your bellies with food and given you luxury. Cattle have built this home and cattle have given you a bank account.'

'Yeah,' Cyn said, still lazily, 'and cattle sent me off to a finishing school that maybe worked in the literal sense instead of the figurative. I've been told that before, too.'

Jim said, 'I fight no farmers, unless they fight me first.'

Old Hans studied him. Jim felt the impact of the old cowman's dull eyes. He wondered what thoughts ran behind those eyes. Would the old rider really move against the cowmen with fire and steel? He was a hard, hard man to read, to understand. He had made his own law for many years. The country was the same, Old Hans Nelson was the same, only the social order had changed. This latter change had not affected the land, for land is impervious to man's thoughts and methods, and land has the last laugh. It had not affected

Old Hans, either. He had intelligence, but he also had a deep Nordic stubbornness.

'Not your father's son.' The cowman shook his head.

'Doc Smith's records say I am,' Jim reminded him.

'Your father was a fighter.'

'Maybe I'm a fighter too.'

'I don't know.'

Jim Clayton had no answer to that.

Cyn glanced at her mother, and her glance said, Tell Dad to lay off. Her mother still seemed interested in the weave of the tablecloth, but Jim knew this was only a pretense and that the housewife was listening to each word. And he knew too that she was worried. And perhaps she had just cause for worry...

'The farmers will hit you too, Jim. You run cattle here, too, and don't ever forget it. Even though your Bar T isn't a big outfit, the farmers will gradually run you out of business.'

'This is no farming land. Drouth and another hard winter will break them and they'll have to leave. Their capital is getting low.'

'What if one came to you for a loan? Would you give it to him?'

Jim had been expecting that question. He

had been hoping it would not arise. But here it was—gaunt and ugly and demanding. He had to answer it.

'Yes, I'd lend him money.' Old Hans started to say something, but Jim held up his hand and got silence. 'I'd lend it to him if he had the proper security.'

'A banker's viewpoint, again. Interest and security.'

'My business, Old Hans.'

'They'll run you out of the cattle business, I warn you.'

'I'll wait for that day.'

'Maybe I won't wait.'

'Dad!' Mrs. Nelson's voice was sharp.

Old Hans glared at his wife and opened his mouth as though to speak, then evidently thought better of it and looked back at Jim Clayton. His eyes held reproach and a bit of anger. And Jim felt a little angry himself.

But he held his anger. Anger had no place here. He and Old Hans were long-time friends; Old Hans had held him as a baby. The old cowman was just hot under the collar at present.

But still it hurt him. When you know an oldster as well as you know your own father—when he has been your friend all your life—well, you don't want to break off your friendship through anger.

Jim looked at Cynthia Nelson. She was looking at him and she seemed to be brooding; her eyes were ageless. She looked at him and did not see him; her eyes held the wisdom and the riddle of all womankind. Or was it just his imagination?

He got the impression—the sinking, sick impression—that they were all standing at the edge of a bottomless abyss and some great force—some unseen force—was slowly pushing them off into eternity.

It was a cold, terrible feeling.

'Good day,' he said, and left.

He found his stirrup through long habit, and the turmoil stayed with him as he put his pony to a wild lope. Cyn's collie followed for a quarter of a mile and then was left in the dust. He stopped and trotted back to the Nelson ranch.

A mile went by on hard hoofs, and then Jim held in his bronc and let the horse slow to a running-walk. He forced his thoughts to settle into a steady mold. This had been a bad day. He had knocked Hal Davis kicking and thereby had made an enemy. True, Davis had forced him to hit him.

Still, Davis was an enemy.

Jim had heard through various channels that some of the farmers were in tough financial shape. That was only logical. Hard winter and a drouth meant no crops, and without crops there was no income.

His mind kept running back to the scene in the Nelson ranch house. Mrs. Nelson was worried, and this worry was plain for him to see. Cyn too was worried, but she wore her worry deep and hid it with a touch of indifference. But yet the worry was there. That was the difference between Cyn and her mother. Mrs. Nelson was direct and Cyn was subtle. Yet when occasion demanded and when something stirred her deeply, Cyn too went directly to her goal and lost her subtlety.

Would Old Hans and his men move against the farmers?

Jim doubted that. Old Hans knew that the farmers were in bad financial shape. Old Hans was nobody's fool. He'd wait and watch and hold in his impatient horse. He had brains. A man doesn't build a big cow outfit without having brains.

He held in his horse, looking to the west. Old Hans had said, '... Your Bar T isn't a big outfit, but you are in this, too...' And Old Hans was right. His bank involved him, and so did his cow outfit. He thought, I'll ride over to the spread and spend the night joshing with Jake.

No, he had business at the bank.

A few miles out of town a rider approached

him, coming from Valley Center. He rode up and said, 'Howdy, young un.'

'Hello, Jake.'

Jake Stone took off his hat and ran his hand across the sweatband. 'Another hot day. I was in town and they told me you had headed out for the Nelson outfit, so I thought I'd ride out and look you up.'

'Something wrong at the ranch?'

'Nothin' wrong.' Jake Stone was squat and tough in his saddle. 'Just friendship, a man might say.' He had a slow smile.

Jim had a touch of irritation. 'I'm over twenty-one,' he said significantly.

'You don't say.'

Jim grinned, his anger leaving.

Jake Stone said, 'Wolf ears, eh?'

Jim told his foreman about killing the two wolves. He also told him about his run-in with the Davis bunch. Jake Stone, he noticed, was about the same build as Hal Davis—stocky and wide and rough. Only Jake was older. Jake was about fifty-five, and Jake had been a good friend of his father's.

'I've seen that girl.'

Jim gave the foreman a quick glance. But Jake Stone was looking at the trail ahead of them and he did not meet his boss' eyes.

'She looks all right, Jim.'

'Why bring that up?'

This time Jake Stone looked up. He spread his hand and made a quick gesture. 'Just a statement.'

They rode into Valley Center. A woman came out of the hotel and stopped on the edge of the plank walk.

'Hello, Jim.'

'Howdy, Miss James.'

Jake Stone lifted his hat. She was dark and small, quick and sharp and keen, and her thin, lovely face showed this. The wind whipped in—the ceaseless wind—and it moved her silk dress, ruffling her white silk blouse. It stirred her dark, smooth hair.

Jim remembered Belle Davis and remembered how the wind had pushed her dress against her. He didn't seem to be able to get the girl out of his mind.

They rode into the Town Stable and went down. Jim let the hostler unsaddle his horse, but Jake Stone ripped the latigo from his cinch and threw his saddle over the rack. They went outside. Linda James was just in the act of entering the Silver Dollar Saloon.

Jake grunted, 'Why the devil does she work in that dive?'

Jim gave his foreman a quick glance. 'She deals faro there, of course.'

'It ain't a good place for a woman. Those other girls in there—they ain't in that joint to play faro. It looks bad for her.'

'You sound worried.'

'Worried, nothing. But she seems to be a danged nice woman, she does. And I don't like it a bit. She's got a reputation to uphold.'

'You still sound worried.'

Jake flung a hard glance at him. 'Oh, shut up, Jim.'

But Jim was thinking about Linda James, too. The saloon wasn't the best place in the world to work. Jake Stone had been correct about the other girls who hung around the Silver Dollar. Maybe Linda James was in their class.

Jim didn't like that idea one bit. There was a gnawing, sneaking suspicion growing, and he hated it.

No, Linda just dealt faro.

And why was he worried about her, anyway?

CHAPTER FOUR

There was a pitcher of beer on the man's desk. Because of the heat beads of sweat clung to the glass pitcher. A hand came in and poured some beer into a glass. Ice made a tinkle.

'Hot day, Muggins.'

Muggins sat on the edge of the desk, for from this point the cat was high enough to look out the window into Valley Center's main street. Muggins said nothing, and the man's hand came out and probed behind the big tomcat's ears. Muggins started to purr.

'Never too hot to purr, eh?'

The man's arm was coatless and his silk shirt was a little damp with sweat. Your eyes followed up the sleeve and came to a pair of thin shoulders. There was a rather thin neck, and then you came to the man's face. The face of land-locator Dan Shepard.

Shepard had a long, almost sad-looking face. His nose was thin and long, his cheekbones high and with sags under them. He was about thirty, and he had seen a lot of space and a lot of life, and this showed in his thin lips. His hands were thin, too, and the fingers were long as they locked around the cool glass of beer.

'Here's to you, Muggins.'

Muggins resumed his chore of looking out the window. Boots came along the sidewalk, their noise coming through the open door of Shepard's office. Shepard listened and tried to guess as to who walked in those boots. It was a game with which he filled idle hours. He had heard that a blind man could finally tell you were coming by the way you walked. He wasn't blind, but he knew that Jim Clayton was one of the men. He knew Jim's long stride. Who the other man was he did not know. He watched the window and his fingers were steady on the cool glass.

The pair moved into the view of the big front window. Clayton was one man and the other was Clayton's foreman, Jake Stone. Jim Clayton glanced at Dan Shepard, and for a moment their eyes met and held and then broke. There was no antipathy in that glance, Shepard decided.

They passed out of the view of the window, passed across the open door, and their boots died in the distance. Dan Shepard turned the beer glass and his thoughts. Loyalty was a great thing. Stone was loyal to Clayton, and that meant a lot.

Who the devil is loyal to me?

Nobody.

Muggins is.

He petted Muggins, and Muggins leaped to the floor with a long bound and walked out the back door in feline coldness. And Dan Shepard thought, A cat is nobody's friend.

Shepard waited and watched and had his thoughts. There came sounds of another person approaching, and he knew this was a woman. He was looking at his beer glass when Linda James entered.

'This, Miss James, is indeed a pleasure.'

Linda sat on his desk, her long dress trailing over the side. She said, 'Sit down, Dan, and rest your blood pressure.'

Shepard sat and kept his thoughts. This woman was a riddle to him. He had made his play and it had netted him nothing so far. For the first time a woman had not cooperated. He felt a little baffled, and with this was a hurt to his vanity. Or did he have the power still to feel a hurt?

'Beer, Linda?'

'A small glass.'

He got the glass from the cupboard in the corner and poured. She turned it and admired the facets in its amber coolness.

She kicked a leg and he admired her slim ankle. Her eyes saw this, but they showed nothing.

'And why are you here, Miss James?'

She said, 'Dan Shepard, do you always mistrust people?'

'I don't follow you.'

She sipped the beer and her eyes were on his.

'I think you do, Dan.'

He moved his shoulders under the silk shirt. Despite the heat he wore a tie.

'All right, you win.'

'Just a visit, Dan.'

'With what purpose behind it?'

Her face softened, and he noticed this; she again became her cynical self. But he had gained a point, and he knew it and she knew it.

'Dan, are you going to fight Jim Clayton?'

'So that is it, eh?'

'I asked a question. I expect an answer.'

He got to his feet and walked to the window and held his beer glass. She turned on the desk, and her dress rustled.

'What does Clayton mean to you?'

She said, 'I might answer that later, Dan.'

He looked out on the main street. A fine main street! Ankle deep with dust that the wind would pick up and lay in the lungs of humans and animals.

He remembered other main streets. They were hard with concrete and feet moved across them continuously night and day. These thoughts clashed in him. But a man had to make a choice. He had to make his bid for power sometime and in some place. And a man never knew the date of his death or the place of his burial. The run was short, and the winner here would have power.

'I won't fight Clayton unless he moves against me.'

She got to her feet and put her hand on his. It was a childish gesture of faith and seemed out of place in view of her occupation and character. It stirred him a little, though he did not know why.

'Thanks, Dan.'

He drank, and his eyes were cynical and worldly over the rim of the glass. 'Jim Clayton has no use for you. There is Cynthia Nelson, you know. She has her eye on him.'

'Maybe you got this sized up wrong.'

'I know when a woman is in love. She has that light step to her walk, and her eyes tell secrets.'

'Dan, you imagine things.'

Get worldly, Linda James; get that hard surface. Look over your table and watch your bets and play your cards close and sing your song harsh and low. The whole thing is a faro game—or a poker game—and what do you have if you win? A woman was meant for a man and she was meant for love. She wants children and her man and she inherits this. Get worldly again, Linda.

'Goodbye, Dan.'

Her hand fell and she walked out. He stood beside the window and watched her pass his office, but she did not look up. Muggins strolled in the back door and took a seat on the desk.

'Muggins, we're all blamed fools.'

Muggins licked his jowls.

Dan Shepard stood and looked out the window, and again he contemplated Valley Center's dust and squalor. But that sight and that thought for some reason was not solid and good, and he went to the corner shelf and took down his spurs. He knelt and buckled on the Kelly star-roweled spurs with their silver-inlaid shanks. He put on a pair of cowhide chaps and buckled them and went out. He carried his Winchester rifle. He went to the livery barn.

'Hot day, Dan,' the hostler said.

Shepard nodded and had no voice. When a man is filled with thoughts and conflicts he does not care for casual conversation. So he merely nodded and went to his bronc. The horse turned in the manger and looked at him, and Shepard put his hand on the bronc's soft nose.

'Good boy.'

He got his kak from the rack and the Navaho blanket went down on the horse's back. A hand came in and smoothed the wrinkles from the heavy woolen blanket. The rest was automatic: the lift of the saddle and the saddle coming down, the cinch swinging on its latigo strap, and then the near latigo going through the ring. Don't pull that catch too tight, Dan Shepard. It's a hot day for a bronc, and a tight cinch is hard on a horse in this weather.

The bit goes next, forcing its port between the grass-stained big teeth. Then the headstall goes over the ears. Then the jawstrap comes in for buckling and you lead the horse outside by his bridle reins.

Shepard let the horse singlefoot down the main street, dust idle and lazy under steel-shod hoofs. He passed his office and saw Muggins sitting on the porch; there was a bit of shade there. My only friend in town is a tomcat, and I doubt if even he is my friend, at that... But a man shapes his life, and when he wants something he makes enemies. That seemed to be an unwritten law.

He sent a glance toward Jim Clayton's bank and tried to judge its strength. What counted was financial backing, and the bank represented money. But it wasn't Clayton's money. It belonged to his depositors. Still, he had control of it, and the control was all a man needed. When a man controlled money he just the same as owned it.

But how strong was the bank? He had heard it was on a safe financial foundation. But a rumor was a rumor and nothing more. A bank statement was a concrete fact. And he had never seen a statement showing the condition of the Valley Center Bank.

The horse kept to a running-walk. The dust

puffed and rose and then settled. The horse took the trail toward the Hal Davis farm.

The sun was falling, heeling toward the rim of the parched, hungry earth; yet the sun held a terrible heat. And land-locator Dan Shepard found himself looking again at the sky. Not a cloud to mar a person's vision, only the thick, heavy blue of the Montana sky. Well, old-timers said it was one of the worst drouths, and it was working his way. Keep away, rain, and let these hoemen starve. And when their bellies get lean and flat they'll come to me and I'll buy them out—deeds and equipment and land—for five cent on the dollar. Or maybe less...

He ran over the set-up again and weighed one item against the other. He had sneaked a march on Jim Clayton and Old Hans Nelson; already his fence enclosed Sunken Springs, and whoever controlled Sunken Springs controlled this basin. Or so he had analyzed. Of course, there was a scattering of waterholes along the bottoms of the creeks, but another year of drouth would suck them and they would be dry.

He had immediately filed a homestead claim on Sunken Springs and then had fenced that area. He had done that even before Jim Clayton or Old Hans Nelson had realized what was happening. He had hit first and he had hit in a vital spot, and so far he was ahead.

He looked across the broad, undulant land. Dry and parched and without moisture, for the drouth was on. He closed his eyes and leaned back against his cantle; he had his hands locked over the flat Mexican horn of the saddle. Bridle reins hung limp and the wind touched the flat planes of his handsome face.

Once buffalo had grazed on tall grass that the wind bent and touched to the damp earth. Then government men with bloody hands and bloody hearts had established tripods, and their guns and rifles had made their gun-sounds. Carcasses had rotted and the stench had been high. So the buffalo had gone and the redman had been starved until his belly was flat and his ribs showed like the ribs of an old, toothless horse that had somehow managed to shift through a long snowy winter. One order had moved against the other, and one had gone down. The older order had bowed. So it was and had been and always would be. The old order had fallen before the new. He was the new: Hans Nelson was the old.

So he went with his head down and his eyes closed, and his horse kept up that smooth gait. Rain would come again, for the world ran in cycles, and when it came his cattle would be fat and rolling and waddling through the tall buffalo grass. Their backs and rumps would be broad and they would be beef to their hocks. There would be a ranch house on Sunken Springs—it would be long, with pillars and a long porch, and below it on the flat would be corrals and the barns and the bunkhouse and the blacksmith shop and the tool-shed. Irrigation was the answer. Water stored in dams, water turned loose into ditches during dry spells, water moving and soaking and seeping across high fields of oats and wheat and barley and alfalfa and clover. And when the wind shifted you would be able to smell the clean sweet smell of alfalfa. The wind would blow and the wind would be cool as it traveled across the irrigated fields.

The world belonged to those with vision. Yes, and with this vision had to be courage and strength and an indomitable will. Yes, and finances, for this world had its foundation in the Dollar. Whether a man liked the idea or disliked it, he had to admit that King Dollar still sat on the throne.

He kept remembering Jim Clayton's Valley Center Bank.

Harsh reality came in. The vision of this basin and its aromas and green fields left before the invasion of reality. He opened his eyes and looked upon the dried bitter earth.

But the vision was only sidetracked

momentarily.

He put his horse to a long lope.

CHAPTER FIVE

The spring wagon bumped over a half-buried rock. The front wheel of the nigh side lifted, settled; the back wheel then had its turn rising and falling. A hand—a feminine hand—clung to the iron rim of the seat for support.

'Hal, don't drive so reckless!'

'Hang on and shut your mouth!'

'Hal, quit talking that way!'

'Quit trying to order me around!'

Nevertheless Hal Davis slowly pulled in the team until the horses walked. Dust puffed from under the wheels; the leaves on the cottonwoods were motionless against the heat; the wild rosebushes had lost their flowers but some of their aroma still scented the hot air.

'Hold the lines, Belle.'

Her firm, dark hands took the two leather lines. He got out his handkerchief and wiped his forehead and the back of his neck, and he cursed the heat with a slowness that was all the more powerful because of its regularity. Belle listened and said nothing as she watched the horse ahead of her move dust.

'That banker hit me awful hard.'

His lip was swollen. It was thick and blue and it felt numb when his tongue touched it.

'You egged him on.'

He grabbed the reins. 'You haven't even brains enough to drive a team, woman. Here, give me them lines.'

'You've got them. And don't start to rib me. I won't take it. You asked for Jim to hit you. You grabbed Jim's shoulder—'

'Jim? Ain't that kind of friendly?'

'Oh, how you talk? Like a fool, you talk! All right, then: I'll say Jim Clayton, not Jim! Now do you feel better, darling brother?'

'That banker has eyes on you.'

'You sound like a jealous suitor and not like my brother. I know you're worried about money and our farm, but, please, Hal, don't take it out on me. You used to be good-natured even though you always have been stubborn. You never acted this mean until you came to this basin.'

For a moment his heavy face held something that looked like pity. But this emotion, whatever its true character, did not last long. For lines moved in again and gave him premature age.

'I'm sorry.'

She looked at him and he saw the deep rim of tears close to the surface. 'Hal, we pull together, or I leave and go into town—and you know I do not want that. You have been mean to Mother too, lately, and I'm ashamed of you. Hurt me, brother, if you have to hurt somebody; please don't hurt Mother, though.'

'I guess I'm just nervous.'

'Things will work out all right.'

'With this blasted drouth! Yes, if we can keep our heads above water. We'll have to have money soon, though.'

'Why don't you see Jim Clayton?'

'See Jim Clayton? Woman, you are an optimist; either that or you've lost your senses. You gettin' addled?'

'Talk with Dan Shepard, then.'

'I have. You know that. It's always, "Stick it out a little longer. The railroad will come through. No, I can't let you have any money right now, but maybe later. After all, I'm just working for the railroad myself."'

'He's looking after Dan Shepard.'

'You don't have to say that twice.'

They came into the yard and the dust was still with them. It lay along the rims of the buggy's box, and the horses' sweaty hides were tinged with its grayness. Hal drove the buggy close to the door of the frame house.

'Hawdy, Mom.'

'Coming, son.'

Mrs. Davis had to use two canes. She was

not old, but the Midwest had warped her and put arthritis into her hands and legs. Her knuckles were swollen and unbending and pain was always with her. Pain had pulled lines into her face and Pain had matured her before her time. This dry climate, coupled with the high altitude, was helping her, though—or so she said. She had the terrible fear of becoming a burden on her son and daughter, and many times she claimed she was the reason that neither had married. To this Hal would smile and shake his head, and Belle would say, 'Mother, dear, please. When the right man comes I'll marry him and not before.'

'Any berries, children?'

'Lots of them, Mother.' Belle kissed her on the forehead. 'No, you go sit down. I'll take them into the house.'

Shrewd eyes went to her son. 'What's wrong with your lip?'

Sister and brother had agreed to fabrication. So the brother told his mother that when he had been tying one of the horses the animal had jerked up his head suddenly to fight a nosefly and the horse had hit him in the mouth. Mrs. Davis nodded and said, 'Noseflies are bad this time of the year.'

'Run the critter to death,' agreed Hal.

Hal and his sister carried the tub of service-berries into the house. The house had three rooms and was so spotless a cowpoke could eat off the floor as a plate. It held feminine touches—gay curtains and a gay spread on the bed, and in Hal's room the furniture was polished, the floor clean. But still poverty poked its head from each corner. The floor should have had rugs and a carpet, the cupboard lacked a fresh coat of paint, the paint on the outer side of the doors and the window-frames was starting to peel as it lost its battle against heat and the wind.

'Oh, those lovely berries.'

Belle looked at her mother. 'They'll make lots of jelly and lots of syrup for hotcakes. But say, we have to unhitch and get the cows. I suppose they're deep in the brush along the crick. They go in the rosebushes to get away from the mosquitoes and flies.'

'I'll get them,' Hal said.

But Belle was adamant. He would unhook and feed the team and get the hay in the manger while she rode after the cows. She got her bay from the barn and rode bareback. The hot wind blew a stray wisp of hair across her damp forehead. Soon the sun would be down. But still the land would be hot until about midnight. The land was a radiator that stored the heat and later released it slowly and grudgingly.

She kept thinking of Jim Clayton. She did not know whether or not to be angry at the young banker. Of course Jim had stampeded their team, almost wrecking their rig. Still, Jim hadn't known she and Hal had been in that coulee picking berries. So it wasn't really his fault.

Then she remembered something, and this something hurt her and made her a little bit afraid of the future. For she remembered the naked fury that had been in her brother's eyes when Jim Clayton had knocked him down. Hal was not one to forget. She decided she would see Jim Clayton the next time she was in town, and that next time would be next Saturday. She would talk to him about Hal, and maybe he and Hal would shake hands. But she knew that was almost a vain hope. Hal was very bullheaded. She was his sister and she knew.

She found the four head of milk cows in the deep brush along a water-hole. Once this creek had been busy as it had pushed and danced toward the river, but now it was glum and sand blew along where once water had danced. Her dog found the cows and took them out, leaping and biting at their tails. They came on the run, bawling against such treatment.

'Here, Mutt.'

Mutt came back obediently, tongue trailing. He trotted beside her horse, for thus he was in the shade. The sun was kissing the land goodbye. The cows went into a line with Bessy leading them. She saw a rider top the ridge, saw the rider silhouetted, and she said, 'That's a woman.' Because it was a woman it would naturally be Cynthia Nelson. Cyn rode where men rode and she rode at any time of the night or day. She was at home in a linecamp or a drawing room. She hated this land, Cyn did, and that hate was apparent. Belle had only talked with Old Hans Nelson's daughter twice, and both times had been Saturdays in town. And the words had been brief. It was always there. The moneyed man's daughter sparing a few words with the farmer's daughter. And very few words at that...

But the rider was not Cyn Nelson. The rider was Linda James. She rode a black horse and her saddle was black hand-tooled leather. Her riding-habit was split buckskin, her blouse was blue silk, and her hat was back, resting against her back and held by the throat strap.

'Hello.'

'How do you do?'

They had never met formally. Linda's reputation was not too spotless around Valley

Center. She worked in a saloon and gambling den, and that alone put her outside the edge of this rural society.

'You're Miss Davis, I believe.'

Belle nodded.

'I'm Linda James.'

'I've seen you around town.' Belle was stiff.

Linda James' laugh was low. 'I guess I have quite a reputation there. Some even confuse me with the girls who work in the back for Ma Fallon. But one has to make a living, you know.'

Belle glanced at the black horse and the expensive riding habit, not to mention the expensive saddle. The trouble with this world was that some people made too much money and there wasn't enough to go around. What was Linda James doing out on this end of the range? Linda seemed to sense that question. She was out for a ride. This was her night off at the Silver Dollar and she had gone for a ride.

'May I ride with you, Miss Davis?'

Belle couldn't turn her down, for her request had been too open. She said yes and they rode along, following the cows. Belle found herself wondering just what her mother would say when she rode into the yard with a woman who gambled and dealt cards in the Silver Dollar Saloon. The saloon had an annex, and Ma Fallon's girls lived in their small rooms in the rear of the place.

Her mother had strict ideas about how a woman should act. A woman's job was in the home taking care of housework and children. A woman should not boss a man; the man should be the boss. Once married she should stick to her man through hell and thunder and rising water.

Rumor had it that Linda James had been married twice and had been divorced. Rumor held a lot of talk about Linda, though. A divorced woman ... a female gambler ... a woman who worked in a saloon with loud profane talk and fighting, drinking men... Belle was a little worried.

Linda and she talked about various things: the drouth, the heat, how crops were getting along—or rather, not getting along. Belle got the impression the gambling-woman was only using this insignificant talk as a screen to cover up the real reason she was riding this range. Either that or as a feeler leading to some question. Finally that question came.

'Where is Mr. Clayton's ranch?'

Belle turned her horse and pointed. They were in sharp contrast. Belle was riding bareback, and she had put on overalls that were faded and dim from many tubbings. Her shirt was of blue chambray, also faded from the tub, and her boots were old and run over and scuffed.

'Over in that direction, Miss James. On Willow Crick. The only ranch over that way.'

'Oh, I see. I was just wondering where it was.'

For some strange reason Belle Davis felt something that was almost jealousy. Why was this brazen heifer looking for Jim Clayton? Was she spending the night over at his ranch, maybe? She didn't like that thought. Well, Jim meant nothing to her... Then she thought, He has money and we need money. But Dan Shepard had money too.

'Well, have to be leaving you, Miss Davis. I'm very glad I met you.'

'Good day.'

There was finality in Belle's voice. But if Linda James detected it her smooth small face did not show this fact. She turned her magnificent black and loped across the flat, and she was going toward Jim Clayton's Bar T outfit.

The brazen hussy...

Belle was glad the saloon-woman had not ridden into the yard with her. Now she would not tell her mother that Linda James had ridden with her. She was remembering Linda's expensive clothes, that costly horse, that high-priced rig. I guess the way you get expensive things is by doing the things good women will not do. Either that or by marrying a man who can buy these things for you. Or working a man around until he buys them.

She was about a mile from home when she met Dan Shepard. His horse was dark with sweat.

'Why, Miss Belle.'

She showed him a sweet smile. 'Belle only, sir; not the miss. Are you looking for somebody?'

He was gallant. His hat came down gracefully; it rested against his wide chest. 'I have found for whom I searched.' Double meaning was thick in his words. 'Now may I ride with you?'

She thought, Your culture is thin, and that is apparent. She said, 'I would be pleased.'

His horse came in close to hers. They joked and laughed and then their broncs came close. His arm went around her shoulders and she did not push it away. He had money and she needed it, and this thought was paramount.

Their broncs stopped, both tired of the heat.

Their horses stood shoulder to shoulder. His arms were tight and he put on the right pressure. She played her cards, using her attractiveness as an ace. His lean, dark face was over hers, and his lips were opened slightly.

'I didn't know—didn't guess—'

She said, 'Don't take too much for granted.'

They broke and he sat back in his saddle and said, 'Now who would think—Belle, you devil, you.'

'I'd best get along.'

'There's no rush.'

'I'm tired.'

She touched her horse with her heels, and he followed. He wanted to get her off the horse, but he knew that the moment had gone. Then he consoled himself that there was a time and a place for each thing, and this time and place had not arrived. So he rode even with her.

His hand found hers and gave it a quick pressure.

'Good girl, Belle.'

She thought, I've got you where I want you... Or did she have him at that point? He was smart. He had known women before and he had known plenty of them. She was very sure of that.

Go easy, Belle Davis.

She was relieved when they rode into the yard.

Hal stood with his milk pails in front of the brush-barn and gave them a long scowl, for the darkness was still with him. He finally acknowledged the presence of Dan Shepard with a few low words and a nod. And Belle, who had long wondered about the true feelings between her brother and the land-locator, got a feeling that Hal held only dislike and disgust and distrust for this well-dressed man.

'You took a long time to bring in the cows, girl.'

'Too much company.' Dan Shepard smiled. He had sunk back into himself again, and he was thoughtful. He had the feeling he had tipped his hand back there when he had kissed Belle; he had shown too much. The closeness of this girl, the feminine feel of her, had, for a moment, got the best of him. But that moment was gone and stored in the storehouse of his memory. The moment held its significance; perhaps the full realization of it would come later. And he was content to have it thus. He was a patient man, for he had long ago learned that patience was an invaluable ally. When the time came he would move. If the occasion demanded violence, then he would move with violence. If it called for a soft tongue and subtlety, then he would be gentle and have guile. Now he smiled and let it go at that. He had this nester where he wanted him. Once before Hal Davis had come and asked for money. He had wanted a loan.

Dan Shepard had not directly denied him this loan. He had hinted about the railroad advancing it and told him to come back within two weeks. Those two weeks were up within a few days. Hal Davis would get no loan. There would be other stalls, other excuses, other pretences. The next winter might have much snow but not much cold weather, and the snow might melt in the spring and renew the soil's moisture, and the summer might have water. There were lots of *mights*, and a man had to take them all into consideration.

If he advanced money to Davis the word would get around and other farmers would demand loans. Yes, *demand* them, not *ask* for them. And his plan called for them leaving and his owning their land and their buildings.

He knew that sooner or later the farmers would get wise to his skulduggery. He felt sure that some of them already mistrusted him. Some hated him for locating them on their particular homesteads. He had met this hate and had sidetracked it by blaming their woes and financial losses onto the drouth. Nature was working with him. Nature was good to him.

'Something I can do for you, Dan?' asked Hal Davis.

Dan Shepard leaned on his saddle's fork. 'You can smile, fellow. It ain't that bad, you know. To use an old saw, it is always darkest before the dawn.'

'Maybe it won't dawn.'

'Daylight always follows darkness.'

Dan Shepard was sure of himself now. He smiled at Belle, and she did not smile back, and he made mental note of this. He thought, You can be broken, you wild filly, and then he realized the goal would not be worth the effort. He had learned long ago that all women—yes, and all men—were variations of the same plot. Only the theme varied, and this variation gave them their individual characteristics. If she made her play she would get what she had coming. He would not chase her. The days had gone and moved and told their stories, and he had learned great patience. But the time was here to move. First he would run against Jim Clayton. He needed Clayton to help him. He would have to get the farmers to hate Clayton, or to get Clayton to hate the farmers.

Just a few more days, Dan Shepard.

'Light your saddle,' Hal said.

Shepard went down and felt the dust under his boots. He was smiling now, for Mrs. Davis was hobbling across the yard toward him. His hat came off, and he bent low and said, 'Good evening, madam. And I hope this day found you getting toward better health.'

'You are gallant, sir.'

CHAPTER SIX

Summer pushed on, as summer does, and autumn was around the corner. Still the drouth hung on with wolfish tenacity. Once there was a shower—it came on an afternoon—and hopes rose. That is, all hopes except those of land-locator Dan Shepard, who stood beside his office window and watched the rain hit the dust of Valley Center's main drag.

'Think it will last long, Dan?'

The words had come from a stocky, middle-aged man who sat on the back legs of his chair there across the room. He had his back against the wall; his chair was balanced. He was a solid man—as solid as Hal Davis—and if a man happened to see him on a moonlight night from a distance and if that man were looking for Hal Davis he would swear that this man was Hal. There were three men of similar build on this range, and those three men were this man and Hal Davis and the Clayton foreman, Jake Stone.

'Hope not, Ike.'

Ike Wilson shrugged. He had nothing tied

into this except his wages, and those wages were paid by Dan Shepard. He had homesteaded on Wishing Rock Creek and the farmers judged him to be just another of their unlucky assembly—they did not know he was on Dan Shepard's payroll.

'As you say, Dan.'

Muggins strolled across the floor, yawned, then jumped onto Ike Wilson's lap. Wilson's gnarled fingers stroked him, and Muggins purred.

'He won't let me pet him like that,' Shepard said.

Wilson sent his boss a slanting glance. 'He's an outcast, he is.'

Shepard was silent. Sometimes he did not understand this man who wore his gun low and who said not a word of his past. He had come up to Shepard right after the land-locator had arrived in Valley Center and had said, 'You need a man like me on your side, Shepard.'

'Why?'

'I've seen this game pulled off before.'

'Where?'

'Does that make a difference?'

Muggins had rubbed against Wilson's leg. A few days before Muggins had also come out of nowhere and made Dan Shepard's office his home.

'You're hired.'

So Ike Wilson had filed papers on the Wishing Rock farm. He had worked in with the farmers and had done his best to stir them to agitation against Old Hans Nelson and Jim Clayton. Get them mad and suspicious of the other guy and then pull the wool over their eyes. That was Dan Shepard's method. An old method, true, but a successful one. Even politicians employed it regularly, and the populace always fell for it. But were the farmers falling?

'The rain is over with.'

And Dan Shepard had been correct. The wind had swept the rain away, and now hot steam lifted from the arid earth. The sun was roasting and hot, and within an hour the earth was dust again. Later that afternoon word came in that the rain, such as it was, had changed to hail and had taken what little crop Hal Davis had.

'Knocked thet man's wheat an' corn an' oats right to the ground, Shepard. What little crop he had is gone.'

'That's tough luck.'

'Right tough, pore kid. An' him with his sister an' mother to feed. Well, heck, I ain't got nothin' myself. Grasshoppers done hit me an' then the drouth finished it. Your own crops is bad.'

'They're nothin' to brag about.'

Somebody had also cut Hal Davis' pasture fence. The farmer was sure that either Old Hans Nelson or some of his Circle S hands had cut that fence, for Circle S cattle had been grazing in the pasture.

Hal Davis had impounded the Nelson cattle and had ridden over to the Circle S and had confronted Old Hans. Old Hans had sworn angrily that neither he nor one of his riders had cut that fence. Davis and the old cowman had tangled horns, and the argument had been hot and heavy. Unseen by the farmer informant, land-locator Dan Shepard had glanced significantly at Ike Wilson.

After the farmer had left the land-locator had said, 'You did a good job, Ike.'

'I aim to please.' A lopsided, crooked, whiskery grin.

Jim Clayton had heard about the wire-cutting episode from nobody else than Cynthia Nelson. He had expressed the idea that maybe Hal Davis' fence had been cut by somebody else. At this Cyn had frowned prettily.

'But who else—beside Dad—would want the fence cut?'

That had Jim stumped, at least outwardly. He had his ideas, though, for he was no knothead bronc. But he kept those ideas from

Cyn. No use tipping his hand. Bad poker policy. And this was a big poker game. Only instead of chips at stake the valley was at stake. That's how serious it looked to him.

'Going to the dance Saturday, Cyn?'

'Yes, with Wad Kenyon.'

'Oh, Wad, eh?' Jim had tried to essay disgust. 'And here I was just on the verge of inviting you. And now you go out with one of your father's cowpokes and slight the town banker.'

Cyn had asked, 'Are we alone?'

'Yes.'

'Well...'

Jim had backed her into the corner beside the safe. Her lips had been warm and sweet, promising much.

'Please, Jim, please.'

He had looked down into her blue eyes and read something there. This had made him step back with a feeling of loathing inside him, and this feeling was directed toward himself.

'Jim, how I hate this damned country.'

'Why don't you leave?'

'Maybe I have a reason for staying.'

'Do you care for me?'

A cock of her head, birdlike, serious, sweet. 'Yes, in a distant way, I guess I do. But if I married you I'd have to stay here in this awful country.' She had whirled, dress swishing; she had made a lovely picture. Her hair was spun gold in the slanting sun and her dress was lacy. The gods had leaned down and kissed her at the moment of her birth. Yes, he had thought, they have kissed her, and they have kissed Belle Davis.

And then he thought of Linda James.

Why think of her, Jim Clayton? She's a dance-hall girl—no, not that—but she works in a saloon and men curse around her and drink. Jim, why do you think of her?

He had walked across the room and he had stood beside the big desk that had belonged to his father. Each man, each woman, is the sum and total of his or her days; this thought was forming in him now. He looked at the desk and thought of his father. A man is part of his mother, part of his father, and the dominating character forms him; his father had been strong.

'What's wrong, Jim?'

'Nothing.'

She had watched and waited. She was smart enough—she never pushed a point. How could he tell her what ran wild inside? Any more than she could ever tell him. You lived two lives. One was secret; the other, your environment, known. But could you tell a person this?

So the night of the dance had come, and a

dance is a big thing in the cow country even today. Cowpokes and hayhands primp and slick up and get out their top broncs and their private bottles. Those lucky enough to get a girl get a buckboard or spring-wagon or buggy and drive into town in grand style with their ladies sitting beside them. Those who stag come on horseback or with the boss in his rig. The dance starts at sunset and breaks up either in fight or with sunup.

Jim had to stag it.

He danced with Cyn and she was close against him, her hair against his cheek, her scent sweet. He liked the feel of her, and she made him think of many things. Yet there was unrest in her. It came out once. She looked at him and her eyes were almost sad.

'I wish Joe had lived.'

Jim shook his head. 'Don't talk of him, please, honey. He was my best friend. I pitched and he played catcher.' Then he caught the significance of her remark which at first had seemed idle and without purpose. Joe Nelson had died when a rope-horse had been jerked down on him. He had been born two years behind his sister and he had been Old Hans' life: the sun and the stars, the air the old cowman breathed, the sight of fat cattle on a slope high with green buffalo grass. But still there was more behind this statement. They finished the dance and each had his thoughts. Now the Nelsons had only their daughter. The sun had moved in on her, the air circulated around her, she was the dream and the vision of old age. Could she leave? Hers was the tragedy.

They finished and Jim said quietly, 'Don't do anything wrong, honey. Come to old Jim Clayton first.'

'Thanks.' She kissed him quickly and took her seat at the bench.

For some unknown reason Jim had glanced at Linda James, who had come to the dance with the owner of the Silver Dollar. Of course there was rumor about Linda and her boss. Linda had seen Cyn kiss Jim. Their glances met shortly, and Linda nodded, but when she looked away her upper teeth were in her bottom lip. This gesture had significance.

Or had Jim just imagined it?

Belle Davis had come to the dance with Mack Tuttle, who ranched on Rock Butte. Jim had danced next with her. Tuttle was a heavy man of the earth, short-coupled and bound domestically to the soil he tilled, and he sent the banker a cold, almost harsh look. It held plenty, although it said little. Farmers had come to Jim for loans but had got not a cent. No security. There was a rumor around that Jim was known among the farmers as No

Security Clayton. The rumour had got to Jim's old bookkeeper who had repeated it. Jim had no place in his life for rumors, and he had smiled it away, for it had hurt him not one iota. A man who followed rumor, in his estimation, was asking for trouble. He was worse than an old maiden aunt surrounded by her kittens.

It didn't hurt him a bit. Therefore the look that Tuttle had sent him did not hurt him. He danced with Belle, and she was distant and cold. He tried to talk to her and got brief but polite answers. He glanced once at her brother. He stood near the doorway and watched them with truculent doggedness. He was drinking, Jim knew. Jim Clayton wanted no trouble; he'd stay away from Hal Davis.

'And how is your mother?'

'She is getting better, thank you.'

She didn't move close against you as Cyn did. Cyn danced with her eyes closed, her lips parted, and her body became a part of yours— it became blended into symphonic music, into liquid rhythm. Jim was almost glad when he led her back to her seat.

'And I thank you, Miss Davis.'

'Thank you, sir.'

He walked away, almost angry. Women had a way of making a man feel cheap and dirty, and they could turn him inside out with just a few ripe words. A voice said, 'You look like you didn't come out too good, Jim.'

Linda James stood there, dark and small, with her thin dark face.

Jim said, 'Can you women always read a man?'

'I can read you, Thunder Cloud.'

Jim said, 'Let's dance.'

Cyn had been smooth but this woman was all movement. You danced with her and you caught her perfume and her body moved against yours. You couldn't remember all the rumors and half-talk you had heard about her. You only wanted to become the main character in those rumors.

The music ended.

'You dance well, Jim.'

'You're no amateur.'

'I have done lots of things, James Clayton.'

Jim read her correctly. 'With the right man, you should add.'

'I've never met the right man yet.'

He believed her. That was odd. She dealt faro in a smoke-filled saloon where men cursed and swore and fought and drank, and back of the saloon were her girls. Some were not girls. Some were almost old women.

'Will you ever meet him?'

'I'll take that back, Jim. I've met him—I'm sure of that—but he's an old dumbbell. He can't see.'

'Get him some specs,' Jim had joked.

He had glanced at Hal Davis, who had just re-entered the hall after taking a drink. Davis was dark and gloomy and a challenge was with him. It was apparent and strong, and Jim blamed it on drink.

He deliberately avoided Hal Davis, for he wanted no trouble with the farmer. Because of this he did not dance again with Belle. He caught her glancing toward him once, and he knew she was wondering why he had not asked her again, and then he knew for sure she was playing the game called Indifference.

He did not get into trouble with Hal. Two days later the farmer came and asked him for a loan. Jim had to turn him down because he had no security.

Davis showed anger.

That night Jim's bank was robbed.

CHAPTER SEVEN

Cynthia Nelson and Old Hans were in Jim's office when Hal Davis entered that day. Davis had been drinking a little at the Silver Dollar and the darkness was on him. The whisky had driven him enough so that he remembered wrongs, both real and imaginary.

Jim had heard the door open, but from his office he could not see who had entered. He had heard Davis say, 'Where's Clayton, clerk?'

'In his office, sir.'

'Office, eh!' Jim had heard the farmer snort. The word *office* had held all the scorn a country-man holds for an office-worker.

Cyn had glanced out the door into the bank proper. 'Hal Davis is out there, Jim,' she had said quietly.

Jim had nodded.

Old Hans had got to his feet. 'We'll leave, Jim, for we have no business here, and you're a busy man.'

They had just been gossiping.

Jim followed them to the front door, nodding at Davis as he went with the Nelsons. Old Hans had given the farmer a nod, too. But rebellion was in Hal Davis and he had not returned the gestures.

Jim had gone outside with the Nelsons for a moment. He had no special desire to talk to Hal Davis. Davis was bull-headed enough when cold sober, and a few drinks swayed him easily. Jim had caught the flat odor of whisky on the farmer's breath when he had walked past Davis.

'Goodby, Jim.'

Cyn's eyes had said things. But Jim did not return her glance. Old Hans mumbled something, looked at the clear sky; the wind sang in the eaves. The endless, always-singing Montana wind. The wind that never stops.

'One day it blows across Montana from Idaho to the Dakotas,' Old Hans said. 'Next day, by gosh, it whistles back toward Idaho, rushin' to get back home. Wonder it doesn't play out the danged soil.'

'Or the people on it,' Jim added.

Old Hans spat, said, 'Don't let that hoeman push you around. He tried to lay the blame for his cut fence on me, the hellion. I never cut his fence. Neither did any of my men.'

'You sure of your men?'

Old Hans had given Jim a sudden glance. 'Sure I'm sure of them, Jim. I'd not hire anything but an honest man.'

'Is there such an animal?' Cyn was scornful.

'The trouble with you,' her father told her, 'is that you're too young to know so much. Come along, kitten.'

'Kitten, eh?'

Jim had gone back into his bank. Davis still stood by the cashier's window. The old cashier said, 'A man to see you, Jim.'

'Come into my office.'

Davis moved ahead of him. His back was wide and he walked with a rolling gait. Jim figured that a few more years and some more whisky would broaden that back still more and add a big belly to the front side of it.

'Any chair, Mr. Davis.'

Davis sat down. He had the uncomfortable attitude of a man in strange surroundings. Jim found his chair and toyed with a paper-weight and waited a little while. Finally he looked up.

'You wanted to see me about some business?'

'What else would we have to talk over?'

'I'd like to have you as a friend.'

'You can't have a man's friendship after you swing on him and knock him down. Friendship can't be bought by money.'

Jim realized they were on the wrong track. Friendship was not a matter to be discussed at this time. So he changed the subject.

'Your business, Mr. Davis?'

Davis wanted to borrow five hundred dollars. He had come prepared. He had the first papers on his homestead, and his only debts were to the Mercantile and the lumber yard. Jim made a mental note that the Merc and the lumber yard had gone all out for the farmers and had extended lots of credit. Credit they could probably never collect. Bad business.

'That's the deal, Clayton.'

Jim leaned back. 'Have you tried to borrow

some other place?'

'I don't like that question.'

'Why?'

'That is my personal business.'

Jim shrugged.

'Do I get a loan?'

Jim shook his head.

'Why not?'

'Inadequate security.'

Hal Davis got to his feet. Anger was red and raw across his thick face. Jim was thinking of Belle, and beyond Hal Davis' sister was Mrs. Davis crippled and sick with arthritis. His answer had not come easily.

'Old No Security Clayton, eh?'

'I've heard that you farmers call me that. It doesn't faze me a bit. Had you proper security I'd have advanced you the sum. But you haven't the security. Your crops are ruined. What the drouth didn't get the hail knocked flat. I'm responsible to the board of chairmen of this bank. If your loan backfired—which it would do—it would be up to me to even it with the board.'

'The devil with you and your board.' Davis was very angry now. 'These banks are rotten things.'

Jim nodded. 'Some are. I agree with you. Some aren't.'

'When you got money they want to lend you

money. When you need money you can't get any. Then the bank gets full of money and what happens?' He answered that question himself. 'The banker runs out with a sackful of dough and heads for Florida or California. He claims his bank is broke. His depositors lose everything they have. He spends the rest of his life spending their money and loafing on the beaches. Is that right, Clayton?'

Jim reminded him that banking had unscrupulous men just as any business had shysters. In his opinion the depositor was not sufficiently protected from unscrupulous bankers. He agreed with Davis and Davis quieted down.

'I'd sure like to advance this sum to you, Mr. Davis. But I just cannot. I wish you farmers would leave the valley.'

'Why? I'll tell you why. So your Bar T cattle and Old Hans Nelson's Circle S stock can continue to use gover'ment land for range. Did you ever pay the gover'ment one cent for grazing privileges?'

Jim shook his head. 'Open range.'

'Yes, it *was* open range. But the Homestead Act was passed, and homesteaders will come in and more fences will go up.'

Again Jim shook his head. 'The drouth,' he said. 'I've spent my whole life here, Davis. This land is marginal land—not enough moisture for dry-land farming, just enough rain to keep grass-roots for cattle grazing. You break the buffalo-grass roots out of this soil and it blows. Your farming experience here has taught you that, man. Look how the fields have blown! Come with me.'

Jim beckoned the farmer to the window. Valley Center's main street was dusty and filled with loose earth.

'Wagon wheels have cut up that road like that. Before you farmers came that road was packed hard, except the trail made by cowboys' horses. This town is full of dust since you farmers came. It blows in every day.'

'What is the answer then?'

'Two things. Either abandon your homesteads or irrigate.'

'Irrigate...' Hal Davis was thoughtful. 'With creeks almost dry, where would water come from for irrigation?' He was cynical again.

'Snow water. Store it in reservoirs each spring. Use it from the creeks first, and when the water level falls there then go back on your reservoirs. Check coulee run-off with check dams.'

'Takes money.'

'Not so much money as it takes hard, hard work.'

Davis nodded, said nothing, and went outside. Anger was with him again, and it sat on his thick shoulders. He stopped once just inside the door and gave the bank a long slow perusal. Jim watched his eyes move across the place—settle on the old bookkeeper, the back door, the ledgers and account books, the safe. Something close to sarcasm came into the man's eyes as he looked at Jim who stood in the doorway.

Then coldly and deliberately, Hal Davis spat toward Jim. The spittle, of course, fell short, hitting the floor. This done, the farmer walked out.

Jim Clayton's face was the color of dull putty. His first impulse was to lunge out at Davis and get him on the sidewalk and try to beat him down. The man's insult had been dirty and apparent. Then cold logic throttled this wild impulse. When the fight was over nobody would be the winner—even the winner was the loser in a fight. And it might lead to guns. For Jim had noticed that Davis had packed a gun that looked almost out of place against his heavy thigh.

Jim's old bookkeeper glanced at Jim, but was silent as he lowered his keys to his books. But Jim noticed his hand trembled on his pen as he made his fine clear figures on the ruled columns.

Jim went into the back room and got the mop. The bookkeeper had mopped that morning and the cloth was still damp. He wiped the spittle up and returned the mop to the back room.

'He was mad, Jim.'

Jim said, 'He'll get over it.'

The old man sat upright on his high stool and gloomily looked at his pen. 'I wonder how this will end?'

'Dan Shepard's behind it.'

'That he is. He's an oily, smooth-talking skunk, he is.'

'Don't disgrace the skunk family, please.'

The old man hobbled to the window. 'He's going into Shepard's office now, Jim. I can see through the window. That farmer Ike Wilson is in with Shepard.'

'Wilson's no farmer.'

'You think he is Shepard's right hand man?'

'Yes, I believe so.'

'Maybe Shepard sicked Davis onto you.'

'You got something there.'

The old man was right. Hal Davis came into Dan Shepard's office and said, 'No soap, men.'

Shepard glanced at Ike Wilson, who winked back. Hal Davis was in a chair, looking at the floor, and he did not see Wilson's wink.

'What did he say?' Shepard wanted to

know.

Hal Davis told them in detail the nature of his conversation with Jim Clayton. He even told about spitting on the bank's floor.

'Wish it would have hit ol' No Security.' He looked up. 'I wish somebody would rob that blasted bank. Then he wouldn't be so high and mighty. He'd be as broke as the rest of us.'

'That would be all right,' Shepard admitted.

Davis said, 'Dan, you gotta lend me some money. I have to have some money. I can't stop at this point. I've got too much invested. I've got to get through this winter and give it a chance again next spring. This dry spell has to break sometime. Next year might be a wet year.'

Shepard felt a touch of anger, but logic made it take a back seat. He allowed his handsome face to get a long thoughtful look. He was almost sad.

'Hal, you sure could have a loan if I had the money. I've tried to get advances from the railroad, but they won't lend a thing. I tell you I've tried and tried and tried, but those big shots won't advance a dime.'

'But they'll charge us double rates to ship our wheat, if and when we get any wheat, and when they run steel through!'

'They're robbers,' Shepard admitted. He was very sad now. He looked at Muggins, who sat beside Ike Wilson on the bench. Muggins seemed to be smiling a feline smile. He regarded Dan Shepard with yellow, lifeless eyes. Shepard looked back at Hal Davis. He had the feeling that Muggins was laughing at him and making fun at him. But he realized it was an odd feeling. Cats didn't laugh at humans, and cats didn't poke fun at them. Or did they?

Hal Davis stood up. He was defeated, but he had expected defeat, and therefore the blow was not strong.

'Well, we'll have beef this winter; I'll see to that.'

'Nelson has some fat steers.' Ike Wilson was smiling. 'I got me one spotted for my winter chawin'. Big roan steer with a froze-off tail. Keep your rifle sights off him, eh?'

'As you say, Ike.'

Shepard said, 'Hal, I'm sorry.'

'Well, if you ain't got it, you ain't got it, an' that's all. You've got quite a bit invested in your farm, too. You got the best location in the valley, though. But you got here ahead of us and you got more brains.'

'You compliment me.'

Hal Davis said, 'So long, men,' and left.

Dan Shepard moved to the window in his

slow way, and he was still very sad. The street was dusty and he noticed this, for he hated the dust. He watched Hal Davis climb onto the seat of the spring-wagon. The farmer turned his team and cramped the rig short. He left town with his team at a trot. More dust. Always dust.

Shepard looked toward the bank. He walked back to his desk and sat down. For some time he sat there and contemplated nothing. Ike Wilson watched and wondered what thoughts his boss had. Shepard's face was sad and there was nothing else there but this sadness—there were no thoughts or life or sunshine. Ike Wilson looked at Muggins. Muggins sat on a chair, front feet curled back, and Muggins watched, too.

Finally Ike Wilson said, 'Well, boss?'

Dan Shepard looked at his hired hand. For a moment it seemed as though Wilson's interruption had startled him and by its suddenness had made him angry. This emotion showed, sneaking in between the harshness of training, and Wilson saw the edge of it before long practice killed it.

Shepard made a motion with his hand. 'He fought with Jim Clayton. There is no love lost between them. Now Jim has turned him down another time.'

Wilson waited. Muggins seemed to wait,

too.

Shepard got to his feet for impatience had touched him. He walked toward Muggins, and the tomcat moved away with feline suspicion. Shepard stopped and Muggins leaped to another chair. He sat there in yellow tawniness.

'We've talked about that bank, Wilson. Can you break that safe?'

'I think so.'

'Are you sure?'

'Purty sure.'

Shepard asked quietly, 'You said once you could get it.'

'I think I can. Safes are like people. They're all different.' This was as close to philosophy as Ike Wilson's limited intelligence would let him stray. 'When?'

'Tonight?'

'They might blame it on Davis.'

'You see the light fast, Ike. Sure they'll blame it on Davis. We could even see that some of the dinero is found on Davis' property.'

'There's the night marshal,' Wilson said.

'An ol' man.'

'He's tough.'

'Time has trimmed him.'

Wilson put his index finger to his bottom lip and watched Muggins. Muggins looked back at him. Wilson moved over and petted the tomcat. Muggins started to purr. The purr was a smooth crackle. Somewhere out on the open range a cow bawled for her calf. The sound was good and brought many pictures to the mind of Dan Shepard. Shepard watched his hireling.

'Tonight then,' Wilson finally said.

Shepard nodded. He broke the pencil and tossed it into the wastepaper basket. Tiny beads of sweat stood on his forehead and his black-shaven jaw. He had not remembered picking that pencil from his desk. Yet he had broken it.

'Tonight. Need any help?'

'Alone. I want to do it alone.'

Shepard nodded.

Wilson rubbed his lip thoughtfully. Shepard played with another pencil. The cow bawled again, and this time the calf answered. Those sounds died and the wind made its noise in the eaves.

And Muggins deliberately yawned.

CHAPTER EIGHT

There had been the scuffle of boots in the darkness, the smash of a pistol, and Jim

Clayton came awake. He snapped out of a sound sleep and he was sitting on the edge of his bed there in the Town Hotel.

More shots, harsh in the darkness; he judged they came from the direction of his bank. He was in his trousers, and he found his boots and put them on without socks. His Colt hung from the post of the bed. One scoop and he had the gunbelt and heavy weapon.

He ran down the hall, buckling on the gun as he traveled. The shots had died, and somewhere a horse neighed in fear. The light in the hall was dim—coming from a kerosene lamp in a high wall-bracket—and shadows danced and lunged against the faded wallpaper of the hall. Jim, though, had no eyes for this as he ran down the hall. The side door opened and he almost ran into the woman who came out.

She wore pajamas and they fit her properly. Even the dim lamplight showed that. For a moment the young banker had only eyes for her.

'What's the matter, Jim?'

He had not known that Linda James had taken a room at the hotel. Then he remembered that she had been boarding at the Ferguson home and the Fergusons had moved out of town yesterday.

'I don't know, Miss Linda. Shots from up

the alley! Sounded like they came from my bank.'

'You be careful, now.'

But Jim was already hurrying down the back stairs. His room was on the top story of the two-storied hotel, and his boots clanged as he ran down the dried fir stairs. He had his gun in his hand.

He heard another shot and the sound was ugly. It split the night; Jim figured the time was about two or three. You could make out the outlines of buildings, but it would be hard to identify a man unless you got right close and peered into his face.

'Hey! Help me!'

Although the voice was filled with pain and fear, he recognized it as belonging to old man Hawkins, the night watchman. It came from the direction of his bank and he ran that way, the Colt out.

He wondered how many seconds had gone by since he had jumped out of bed. He knew he had acted fast. He was pretty sure his bank had been held up. Either that or somebody had tried to rob the Mercantile or the saddle-shop.

'Gimme a hand!'

Old man Hawkins' voice again, coming out of the dark. Again the horse neighed in fear, and Jim knew somebody would have a hard time mounting the animal. The neigh told him that. The horse was in pain. Jim knew horses. He had been raised around horses. He had a hunch that bronc had stopped a bullet.

'Who goes?'

The voice was harsh and came from his right. Jim swung his gun on the man and said, 'Jim Clayton.'

'Jake Stone, Jim.'

Jim said, 'There's something wrong at the bank. That was Hawkins who hollered. There goes another shot.'

'Rider over yonder, Jim.'

The man came fast toward them. He was a dark shadow in the darkness. Jim caught the width of him and saw he was stocky. Then the rider saw him and Jake Stone, and the man's gun talked as he skidded his bronc around a corner.

Jim was on one knee, shooting. Jake Stone snapped a shot, too. Then the rider was gone and the roar of his hoofs ran out. Men and women were moving in Valley Center. Doors were banging open. Men and women and children were hollering. Dogs barked and a cat scooted across the alley, tail up. The cat passed right in front of Jim, who still knelt there in the dust. And Jim saw the cat was Muggins.

Muggins clawed onto the top of a shed and

was gone. Jake Stone said, 'He's gettin' away, Jim. Jim, let's get after him!'

'I can't.'

'Why not?'

'My leg. My right thigh.'

Jake Stone went to his knees beside his boss. 'Man, you stopped one, eh? I didn't know it.'

'Lucky shot.'

Jim's voice was suddenly dim. When a .45 slug hits you there's shock, too. A big hand smashes into you and you feel sick and you want to die. Jim had sweat on his face, and yet the morning was cool; there was blood on his leg. He could feel it run down his leg. He thought, My pants will get all bloody, but that was a foolish thought. Yet when a man stops a slug he gets foolish thoughts. He tried to get up and he couldn't. He had a hot poker in his thigh and somebody was turning it. He clenched his teeth and made balls of his hands, but the poker was still red and burning. He thought for a while he would faint, but he kept conscious with an effort.

Jake Stone bellowed, 'Jim Clayton is shot. Get Doc Smith quick!'

Somebody bellowed back, 'They got ol' Hawkins, too. But he's dead. Plumb dead, shot above the heart! Say, where the devil is Doc Smith?'

'Somebody robbed the bank,' a voice hollered.

Jim put his head down. Suddenly he remembered Hal Davis standing there in the bank. He remembered the stocky farmer's slow gaze going over the safe. He compared this memory with the memory of the rider who had just shot and wounded him. That rider had been wide and heavy too.

He thought of Belle Davis, and of Mrs. Davis. Then he was aware that somebody was kneeling at his right side, and he looked up. He wished he could have seen Linda James' thin face. He could not see it because of the darkness, but he thought he read something in the tone of her voice.

'Jim, where did you get shot?'

He had a joke. It helped relieve the tension and the pain. For the poker had lost some of its heat by now.

'In the alley.'

'You big oaf!' Her voice was husky. 'Quit your joking. You know full well what I mean!'

'In the thigh. Right.'

Jake Stone growled, 'Where the blazes is that medico?' and went toward the bank.

Townsmen surrounded them now. One man said, 'Doc is looking at ol' Hawkins.'

'Thought somebody said he was dead,' Jim said.

'He isn't, not yet. Thet gent just run off at the mouth too fast. Hawkins laid there like he was done in, though.'

Jim waited. Except for hushed questions and answers of newcomers, the crowd was silent. Even the dogs had stopped barking. Somebody was on the other side of him, and he recognized Belle Davis.

'What are you doing in town?'

The question was out of place. But Jim Clayton's mind was none too clear. It demanded simple answers to simple questions.

'I stayed in with Jacqueline Easton,' the girl said quietly. 'Doc sent me over here to look at you. They are taking Mr. Hawkins into Doctor Smith's office and then the stretcher is coming back for you.'

'I can walk.'

'Maybe you can walk, but you're not going to try. You just remain in the position you are in, please.'

'My bank—'

'Don't worry about your bank.'

'You sound like you have authority.'

'Doctor Smith asked me to watch over you until he got here. This job isn't of my free choice, if you must know. You see, I'm a nurse.'

'Oh, I didn't know that.'

Linda James said, 'May I help you, Miss Davis?'

'Yes, but there is little we can do, except stop the flow of blood. Who has a pocket knife, please?'

'I have.'

Jim looked up at the speaker. He could not clearly see Dan Shepard's face. Just then Jake Stone came up. According to Hawkins—and the old man had been able to gasp out only a few words—a lone rider had held up the Valley Center Bank. Hawkins had jumped him as he came out the back door with a sack. He had shot the watchman down and they had exchanged shots.

'Did Hawkins recognize him?' Dan Shepard asked the question.

'He didn't, he said.'

Shepard said, 'That is tough luck. Well, we got to get a posse and hit out, men. Move fast now.'

'What can we do in this dark?' a townsman grumbled.

Shepard said they could split up and comb the range. Jim mentioned that he had heard the bandit's horse neigh in pain. He had an idea that the bronc had stopped a bullet. This theory was substantiated by a townsman who said he saw blood on the dust.

'Maybe it was Hawkins' blood,' a man said.

No, the blood had been up the alley, and Hawkins had not got that far from the bank. Jim thought, Look for a wounded bronc, and moved a little.

'Be still, please,' Belle Davis said.

Belle and Linda James had slit off Jim's pant leg. Belle had a scarf tied around the wound, and when she tightened it Jim gritted in pain. She had a short stick stuck under the knot, and she twisted.

'You trying to twist my leg off?'

'Be quiet, foolish.'

Men were moving off toward the barns. Horses made their sounds, and a dog barked and horses moved. Jim heard Dan Shepard barking out orders. This ended, and horses ran out of town and into the distance. Jake Stone had gone back to the bank to check the extent of the robbery. Jim had the money insured to about forty percent, and that would help some. But it would be hard on his bank. He remembered his father and how proud the Old Man had been of his bank. Well, he'd make a go of it, some way. That safe must have been a hard one to crack. An experienced safe-cracker must have cracked it, because he would have to use soup, Jim figured. But he didn't know much about robbing safes. He had read a little on it, but that was all. And since his graduation from Montana U he had learned that there was a wide gap between theory and practice.

Tough luck had hit him. He figured he would be crippled up for some days. Well, he would get around on crutches. The loss of dinero from his bank hurt him as much as did his wound. Only one was physical and the other mental. He wasn't selfish, and a dollar to him was just another dollar. But his father had been proud of the bank he had built. He had passed this pride into Jim. Jim figured he owed allegiance to his directors, too, although he personally controlled sixty-seven percent of the bank. Old Hans Nelson was the other big stockholder. Hans owned about twenty-eight percent. The remainder was divided among other valley residents.

Who had robbed the bank? He again remembered the rider drifting across the night, and he remembered how his gun had matched the strident pound of his get-away bronc's hoofs. A wide man whose face had been hidden by the silent ally of the night. Jim remembered walking into his office with the broad back of Hal Davis ahead of him. He didn't like that thought. He didn't like to think of Davis as a bank robber. And why? Davis hated him. He had knocked the farmer down, and that had hurt the wide man's pride. A blow to a man's pride is sometimes greater than a blow to his solar plexus. He had to turn down Davis' demand for a loan. This had hit the farmer in the pocketbook. And when you hit a man in his pride and then cripple his pocketbook, you smash him in his two most vulnerable spots.

But luck had been with him to a small degree. Old man Hawkins was not dead, and the old man might have identified the robber, although he realized this was doubtful because of the night.

Well, time would tell.

'Here comes the doctor,' Linda James said.

Doc Smith was a pot-bellied old man who would have retired years before had he had some other medico to take his place. As it was, he was close to eighty. He knew this cow-country and everybody in it, and many of the men and women who inhabited this range had first seen the light of day through the efforts of Doc Smith. He was gruff, but the gruffness was just a mask.

'You danged fool, Jim, why didn't you stay home in bed? Nobody ever gets shot in bed.'

'Had a friend who got shot in bed.'

'How?'

'Whisky bottle.'

'You mean half shot.' Doc Smith spoke to Belle. 'How is he, Miss Davis?'

Belle had the tourniquet in place. Yes, he

could be moved. While the four men held the stretcher, Doc Smith and Belle, aided by Linda James, got Jim onto the canvas. And when Jim lay back he was weak and sick and he almost passed out.

In fact, things did black out for a spell, but it must have been just for a few moments, for the next thing he remembered was the movement of the stretcher as they carried him. It seemed as if he were riding on an ocean boat. Three years ago Montana had gone down to play football with California, and Jim and the others had crossed the Golden Gate on the ferry. The deck of the ferry had moved like this stretcher. Jim lay back and closed his eyes.

Somebody said, 'Be careful.'

They were carrying him into the hotel. Jake Stone walked beside his boss, and the lamp in the lobby showed the worry of the man. Jake said, 'I got the door shut. He jimmied it. The safe door was wide open. Didn't look like he used powder, either. Somebody sure knew how to crack a bank.'

'Maybe it was a safe-cracker just passing through,' Jim advanced.

Doc asked, 'Where's his room?'

The woman who owned the hotel told them to put Jim in Number 7, which was downstairs. She would have his belongings moved down, but it was best not to try to get him up the stairs. Old Hawkins was in 7, Jim found out, for when they carried him in the old gent lay on a single bed and looked at him.

'So they got you, too, button?'

'Who was he?'

The room had suddenly become very quiet. Jake Stone looked carefully at Hawkins; he peered at him, and his face was set. Doc Smith stood silent. Linda James and Belle Davis were also quiet. Old Hawkins did not answer right away.

Dan Shepard asked, 'Did you get to see him, old man?'

Hawkins spoke slowly. 'No,' he said, 'I didn't recognize him.' He closed his eyes, and his lids were thin over his sunken eyes. His face was quiet and without thought, and death seemed near.

Jim became suddenly sick, and he vomited. They thought it was because of his wound, but actually the spasm was brought about by the death-like whiteness of the old watchman's thin face. He had known Hawkins all his life. Hawkins had raised a big family and his boys had been Jim's friends. They had all left this region. Mrs. Hawkins had died about the time Jim's mother had passed on. Hawkins had raised his family alone. He was a good man, a member of the local church; he took an occasional drink and he always had a good word for everone. He was smart enough, too. Jim had been the main cog in getting him on as night marshal. Jim had pull at the county-seat and he had used his pull. Old Hawkins was too proud to ask for aid from his family or his county. Jim knew personally that his boys and his two daughters occasionally sent him money. He knew, too, that most of this was sent back.

'They've got families, Jim, an' they need their few dollars for shoes an' clothes an' warm chuck for their little bellies. Me, I'm just an ol' goat; why, I can chew on tin cans down in the dump.'

Then Jim had got him appointed night watchman.

Jim lay and thought as they worked on his leg. Good for a man to have thoughts at a time like this. He knew his leg was not broken. His wound was just a flesh wound; Belle Davis had said the bullet had passed right through. That seemed odd: the whole thing seemed crazy. Here he suspected Hal Davis, and Hal's sister had taken care of him and would probably nurse him and old man Hawkins. Irony there. Jim remembered when he had first met Belle Davis. His horse had come on the run and she had been in his way. He remembered the wind and her dress buffeted by the wind; he remembered her wind-rumpled hair and her girlishness. You meet strangers, and some play a big part in your life; others amount to nothing.

'How you comin' along, Jimmer boy?' That was old Hawkins.

'I'll live, Hawk.'

Old Hawk winked. 'Good boy, Jimmer. Good boy.'

CHAPTER NINE

Boots moved across the pine flooring. They made their noises and they continued rising and falling. They were big boots—Justin boots. They were scuffed and the heels were run-over and they had thick soles. The spurs were silver-mounted with hearts and aces along the shanks, but these were dim and needed polishing. The uppers were creased and sagging. Your eyes went upward and the man's legs were thick and solid, and his torso was like that of a large tree. He had a thick chest and his arms were powerful. He stopped and listened. His attitude was one of wariness and suspense. A horse had come into the alley and stopped. The man waited, and he seemed to be a wild animal expecting danger.

He listened to the boots come. His tongue came out and wet his parched lips as he waited. The boots came closer, and the rear door opened, and then wariness left the man.

'Howdy, Dan.'

Dan Shepard threw his hat onto a chair. He went to the window and looked out, and the man watched the land-locator's almost sad face. Dawn was high now and turning into early forenoon. Shepard gave the street a long, careful glance and then turned and spoke to Ike Wilson.

'Well, Ike?'

Wilson asked, 'Could anybody hear us talk?' He was wary again.

Shepard went to the rear door and looked at his bronc standing in the alley. 'Nobody can hear us. Nobody at the back or the front. You did all right, Ike. For a while I thought maybe you had stopped a slug. There was blood on the alley dust.'

'Not mine.'

Muggins got off his chair and rubbed against Ike Wilson's leg. He purred so loudly that you could hear him crackle.

'The horse's blood,' Ike Wilson said. 'I hit somebody. I'm sure of that. Must've been the night watchman, the ol' fool. He come outa nowhere and jumped me just as I was makin' my break. I wonder if he recognized me?'

'No.'

'You sure?'

'So he says. He's wounded bad, too. But the best part of it was that you nailed the banker, too.'

'No!'

'You danged right, Ike. Remember throwing some shots at those two men who shot at you?'

'Dang it, they come outa nowhere, too. So one of them was the tinhorn, eh? Did I salt him down permanent?'

'Just wounded him. Right thigh.'

The boots moved again; the rowels made their sounds; the heels lifted and fell. They stopped suddenly.

'Dan, everythin' is all right then?'

Dan Shepard sat in his chair with his legs wide ahead of him and he sadly contemplated the toes of his boots as if the Justins held a sudden interest to him. He sat that way for a full minute, and Ike Wilson watched him. Shepard weighed this problem, matching the pros against the cons, and Wilson watched and tried to read the verdict on this man's thoughtful face. Shepard was lean and hard and he could use a gun and he could use his brains. Wilson could use a gun, but he was short on brains. Wilson knew this, and therefore he watched in silence.

'All safe on all bases, Ike.'

Wilson talked in a low voice. The safe had presented difficulties. It had had a better lock than he had figured. But he had worked and opened it without using powder. He would have had a cinch had not old man Hawkins blundered on the scene just as he was climbing onto Hal Davis' horse.

'The ol' man recognize the horse as belongin' to Davis?'

Shepard shook his head.

Wilson continued. The horse had stopped a slug that had creased his left rump. It had slowed him down a little but not too much. He had headed back toward the badlands where his own bronc had been tied, and he had turned Davis' horse loose there and had ridden back on his own cayuse. He figured that nobody had seen him until he had ridden into town and then Mrs. Carter had seen him ride into Valley Center. She had been sweeping her back porch when he had come down the alley.

'She'll figure you were out with the posse and came in early,' Shepard remarked. 'No, Ike, we're stony clear, we are. Walk the streets in peace.'

'It all depends on ol' man Hawkins.'

'Why?'

'He might have seen me. He might know

who held up that bank. I had a mask, but it cut off my wind and I figured I wouldn't need it, so I let it slip down.'

'If he'd recognized you he'd have said so, wouldn't he?'

Ike Wilson cocked his heavy head. 'Yes, that's right. Well, it worked out all right, even if that ol' fool watchman blundered on me. I know those other two—the banker an' that gent with him—didn't catch my face. I had my mask up by that time. An' they were a long ways off.' He rubbed his palms and chuckled. 'An' I got the banker an' that was good luck. I hate that son.'

'I don't love him myself. Go on and tell me more.'

Well, Ike Wilson had left Davis' stolen bronc in the badlands, had thrown his saddle on his own cayuse and ridden into town. But on the way out to the badland camp he had sneaked into the Davis barn.

'Hid some of the stolen money in the farmer's hay, Dan. You want that farm of his, an' with him in the clink he'll want money for a lawyer and you'll get the spread for a lawyer's fee.'

Shepard smiled.

The remainder of the money was hidden at a prearranged spot out in the rough country. There would be a time when they could get it and use it, but that time was not now. Wilson wondered if the bank had a record of the numbers of the big bills. Some he said were in a thousand-dollar denominations, others in hundreds and smaller. He judged that he had lifted about thirty thousand dollars. He had left about a thousand in the hay in the Davis barn.

'They'll find that bronc in the badlands and figure Davis hid him out there and hiked home. The shack was dark when I come in.'

Shepard said, 'We'll see, Ike.'

By noon the range was in a state of excitement. Farmers came into town and Valley Center was filled with local people. The sheriff came over from the county seat and he had three deputies with him. By this time the posses had returned to town. The men had split up and each group had found nothing. Old man Hawkins was in a coma. One farmer said he was in a comma. Dan Shepard smiled at this display of ignorance. Dan Shepard kept his eyes open, his mouth shut, and he had an ear to the ground. Ike Wilson played the role of a farmer. He moved from group to group and listened and said little. Gradually he became satisfied that Hawkins had not recognized him. He tried to visit with Hawkins and Jim Clayton, but Doc Smith would let nobody but Linda James and Belle

Davis into Number 7.

'Hawkins is in too bad a shape to have a visitor, Wilson. And besides, what do you want to see him about?'

'I had all the dinero I own in this world in that bank, Doc.' This was true in one sense: Ike Wilson had had about two hundred dollars in the bank. But it had not been all the money 'he owned in this world,' as he had said. 'I thought there might be an outside chance Hawkins had recognized that bandit. I want to hunt him down an' get my money back.'

Doc Smith had assured him that old man Hawkins had not recognized the bandit. Hawkins had repeated that time and time again. No, Jim Clayton and Jake Stone had not recognized him, either.

'Have the authorities got any clues?'

'Yes, I just got word the sheriff has arrested Hal Davis.'

'Hal Davis! Why, thet farmer wouldn't harm a angleworm, he's thet gentle. I don't understan' all of this, Doc.'

'I don't either. But I just heard that.'

* * *

The whole country was surprised. But one of the sheriff's deputies—a man named Hank Jones—had found Hal Davis' saddlehorse back in the rough country. The horse had a wound across his rump. The deputy figured that wound had been caused by a bullet. He had talked it over with his boss and the other deputy. The result was a secret raid on the Davis farm. Hal had admitted that the horse was his. There was no use lying, for the bronc carried his brand. He claimed ignorance and wondered how the bronc got into the badlands. The horse had been missing from his pasture. He had looked for him but had not been able to find him. And here the deputies had found him and he had a bullet-wound!

The other deputy—a man named Will Lawson—had found some money cached where Ike Wilson had hid it. They had tried to get a confession from Davis, but he maintained he had not hidden the money. He argued that had he robbed the bank he would have shot the bronc and killed him and buried him to get him out of the way. The sheriff had the theory that Davis had figured nobody would find the bronc and the wound would heal quickly, and Davis would have a well horse and be beyond the range of suspicion.

So the entire rangeland was surprised—that is, the entire rangeland with the exception of Ike Wilson and land-locator Dan Shepard. These two feigned surprise, though; they listened and watched and waited and weighed each new turn of this wheel.

Jim Clayton was surprised, too. He was not surprised that the robbery was blamed on Hal Davis, though. He was surprised that Davis had been such a fool as not to get rid of the get-away bronc permanently. That, to him, was the fly in the soup. He ran it through a mental sieve and still the fly persisted.

Cyn Nelson brought the news to him. Her face was flushed, for the sun was hot and her ride had been hard and long, since the deputies and the sheriff had stopped at the Circle S before coming into Valley Center. Therefore Jim had been the first man in town to know that Hal Davis was under arrest and charged with bank robbery.

Jim watched the animation sweep across her face and give it color and beauty and a touch of excitement. When she had finished with her story he questioned her and then said, 'Bend down, kid.'

'Why?'

'You know why...'

'Jim, I'm going to quit kissing you. One kiss will lead to another and the first thing you know I'll be in love.'

'Won't that be fun?'

'For you, yes. But how about me?'

'You'll enjoy it.'

She did not blush. 'Maybe I've fallen in love already.'

Her head came down and her lips met his. His arm went around her back and pressed her down. She left her chair and got on her knees beside the bed. He didn't know just how to regard her—one time she was just like a sister and the next she was his sweetheart.

With one eye he saw the door open. Belle Davis' brown hair showed and then came her sweet face. She said, 'Oh,' and the door went shut with a bang. Only then did Cyn lift her head.

'Who was that?'

For some reason Jim fibbed. 'Doc Smith.'

'Nice of him to leave us alone. Jim, I don't know whether I love you or hate you. You have designs on me.'

'They're all evil.'

'I know that.' She was very serious. Then she broke out with, 'Oh, how I loathe this country, Jim, and its stupid people. Jim, I'm going to the University of Chicago this fall.'

'I thought you were out of college.'

'I am. I'm going to do graduate work.'

Jim looked at the ceiling. He was still in a turmoil. He didn't know what to think or to say. She watched him closely for the effect of her words. Finally he said, 'I'll miss you. But maybe it is for the best.'

'You got the nester girl.'

'Don't be spiteful.'

She got to her feet and smoothed her buckskin riding skirt. Her silk blouse lifted and fell.

'I haven't left yet.'

After she had gone Jim cupped his hand behind his head and gave this problem some thought. When he was close to her he thought he loved her, and when they were apart he seldom thought of her. He remembered the surprised look in Belle Davis' eyes when she had looked in and had seen him kissing Cyn Nelson.

Where did Belle fit into this?

Belle would take the news of her brother's arrest very hard. He was sure of that. Naturally she thought a lot of her brother. The Davis family, he had guessed, was a close group. He had caught that impression many, many times. This would be tough on Mrs. Davis, crippled as she was. Jim rolled over. His leg pained him a little, but the wound was draining well and Doc Smith said he could get up on crutches in about two days. Jim was impatient, of course. He had always been on his feet, and now that he was confined to a bed he was indeed restless. They had moved him back to his old room. Old man Hawkins had been too sick to share his room with a fellow sufferer who was not in such pain. Therefore the doc and Belle had moved Jim back to his old room. He felt better here, too. More at home.

When the door next opened he expected Belle to enter, but instead Linda James came into the room. Jim had a wry thought: Linda was the only one in the trio he had not made a play for. Now why did he think of that? In fact, why was Linda James staying in Valley Center? Sure, she ran a faro table in the Silver Dollar, but there was little gambling or drinking in this town. Farmers were too poor to gamble and cowboys made darned little money. Jim wondered why she did not go over to Zortman or Landusky in the Little Rockies to the southwest. The gold fields over there were booming. She could make more in one night there than she could here in a week. He had heard that Ma Fallon was considering moving her girls and belongings over to the mining towns. There was lot of conjecture about Ma. There was a lot of gossip about Linda, too.

Jim said, 'Hello, Miss James.'

'Have you heard the news about Hal Davis' arrest?'

'Cyn Nelson just left. She told me.'

'Oh. I saw her on the street. They just brought Mr. Davis into town. I feel sorry for his sick mother.'

'And his sister, too.'

'Oh, yes, his sister, too. And how are you today, Jim?'

Jim complained because Doc Smith would not let him get on his feet. She sat and held her pocketbook on her lap. She had on black—a pert black hat on her dark, sleek hair, a black dress and black stockings and black shoes. Only her blouse was white, and it was sleek and silken. The black dress clung to her long, slender body. She looked very pretty and very nice. Jim found himself telling Jim Clayton that, Heck, just because she works in a saloon isn't any sign she isn't a nice woman. Now why did he assure himself thus?

'Be up and around in two days, Doc Smith says. Me, I figure sure I could get up now, if I had some crutches.'

'You'd best do as Doc says. You have a good nurse, so take your time.'

Good nurse... Jim wondered if there were not some subtle sarcasm in that statement. A woman was something he could never understand. One moment they purred like a contented kitten and the next they clawed like a cornered bobcat. He decided to skip the whole issue.

'She's a good nurse, Miss James.'

Linda James got to her feet and smoothed

her black dress. She asked if there were anything that she could do for him, and he said he couldn't think of a thing. So she said goodby and left. Jim listened to her going down the hall and down the steps and he thought, She sure has good breeding and good manners. She was no rowdy like Cyn, dang her beautiful bones. Nor was she as straightforward as Belle. But all nurses, he had heard, were straightforward.

He hated to have to meet Belle face to face again. It hurt him a lot more than he had expected. She thought heaps of her brother, and when a girl's brother is accused of robbing your bank and she is your nurse—But when the girl came with Doc Smith she gave no clue that she was disturbed. Only her hurried, quick movements gave an indication of her inner turmoil.

Doc was gruff as he worked, swearing now and then, spitting tobacco juice out the window. Jim wondered how the tobacco juice could keep from hitting passers-by. But he heard no curses or yelps of anger, so he guessed nobody had been hit by the liquid streams that emitted from Doc Smith's thick jowls.

'Be up in two days, Jim. Now take it easy and rest, son. You going to stay with him awhile, Miss Davis?'

Both looked at Belle. Jim couldn't understand just why Doc had asked his question. Then it dawned on him that the doctor wanted him and Belle to be alone so they could talk over this sudden trouble confronting the girl. Doc Smith was reading a lot into this and it all spelled LOVE. Maybe Doc Smith was getting out of the realm of medicine and maybe it darned right was none of his business! But when a man gets old and doddering—

'He has no further need for me, Doctor Smith.'

Doc Smith grunted something, and he and Belle left. She turned at the door and glanced at Jim. She had not expected him to be watching her, but he was. And for a moment, her deep mask of self-control slipped just enough to show him her fear and worry and heart sickness.

Then the door closed and she and the doctor were gone. Jim Clayton lay on his back, and he was very, very sober. An ant came out of the moulding and started his long trip across the ceiling.

'Get back there, you fool ant!'

The ant kept on walking.

CHAPTER TEN

The next day they held a preliminary hearing for Hal Davis. The trial was held in the hotel lobby and it was crowded to the brim, so Jake Stone later told Jim Clayton. Even Mrs. Davis, bent, stooped, got into town for the trial. Jim had not seen Belle since she had left the day before with Doc Smith. Doc had told him this morning that Belle had quit her job.

'Shucks, you don't say.'

'Guess she couldn't take it, son.'

'I sure feel sorry for her, Doc. Yes, and for her old mother, too. Wish those farmers would pull out of this country. Man, the dust is sure blowing today, isn't it, though! Look at it come in from that window! Guess you'll have to close it, Doc.'

'Be awful hot and stuffy in here with that window closed.'

'I'd rather die from heat than be choked to death by the dust.'

Doc closed the window and stood for a moment looking out of the dust-smeared pane.

'When your daddy and Old Hans Nelson trailed Texas cattle into this country, the whole range was buffalo grass that had roots spread out and so tight they held the soil down when the wind blew hard, and the wind always blows hard here. Your daddy always claimed that when the hoofs of cattle wore paths this dust always blew. He and Old Hans said that when hoofs broke the buffalo grass roots, the wind lifted the dust.

'Now the plow has come in and broken those roots and the land is moving in the dust all the time. God, I'm tired of dust, Jim! What is the answer?'

'Irrigation, for one thing. Keep the soil moist and let alfalfa grow and break the wind.'

'These farmers aren't that smart, Jim.'

'They aren't, but Dan Shepard is that smart.'

Their eyes met and held, the clear young eyes of Jim Clayton and the sunken seamed eyes of old Doc Smith.

'Shepard is the snake in the weeds, Jim. I'm sure of that.'

Jim said, 'We need proof.'

Doc stopped with his hand on the doorknob. 'Davis came into your bank for a loan. You refused him and he got mad. He spit at you and walked out. But first your bookkeeper says he looked carefully at the safe.'

Jim nodded.

Doc turned and said, 'Evidence against

him. Strong evidence. A man of Davis' build robs the bank. The law finds Davis' top bronc wounded and hidden out. The law finds stolen money in the Davis hay.'

Jim watched the old medico.

'What do you say, Jim?'

'Too patent. Too much slick.'

Doc Smith nodded. 'You might have a point there.'

'Where does it put me?' Jim asked.

Doc Smith looked at him. 'Do you have to ask that, Jim?'

Jim had no answer to that. The medico left, and his tread was heavy. But the young banker paid the foot sounds no attention. Doc Smith's answer had been indirect, but yet it had told Jim much. The farmers hated him now more than ever. His bank had been robbed and evidence pointed toward one of their members. Belle Davis hated him. While he had not been responsible for jailing her brother, the fact still remained, cold and harsh, that her brother was in jail for robbing his bank. Jim wished he could walk downstairs and get in on the trial. Then he realized his evidence against Davis would be overwhelming. All circumstantial, but still big and damning. As it was, he listened for the trial, for the sounds came up clearly through the network of the heat register in the floor.

Ed Winchester, who owned the Valley Center Saddle Shop, was the local justice-of-peace, and what he knew about the letter of the law left much to be desired. He chewed tobacco and spat on the floor despite the fact that the owner of the Town Hotel had placed a spittoon beside the judge's chair.

'Court'll come to order,' Jim heard the old saddlemaker say brusquely.

The big lobby became silent. Jim lay with his eyes closed and his ears straining, for the sounds were not too clear through the mesh register. He heard the pound of Judge Winchester's home-made gavel on the plank bench.

'Mr. Davis, sir, stand up.'

Davis evidently had no lawyer. The county attorney—a sleek-eared gent—was in town to represent what he called 'the good and true people of Beaver county.' Judge Winchester droned off the charge against Davis: robbing and making forceful entry into the Valley Center Bank, shooting watchman Hawkins—for the first time Jim found out that old man Hawkins' given name was Elmer—and for this and that, and this and that.

'Do you plead guilty or not guilty?'

'Not guilty.'

Jim heard Winchester say, 'Ain't you forgettin' the proper form of address, prisoner?'

'Not guilty, *Your Honor.*'

Winchester appealed to the county attorney. 'He claims he ain't guilty. Now what does I do, lawyer?'

'Bind him over for the fall term of court.'

This Judge Winchester did. Jim heard Davis ask if he could have bail. At this point the county attorney cut in and said a charge of murder had been lodged against him, Hal Davis, and such a charge was so serious no bail would be allowed. The sheriff would have to take Hal Davis to the county jail and hold him there until his trial was over with. Davis objected strenuously to this. He had his mother and sister to look after; he had his farm to take care of.

The county attorney said, 'You should have thought of that, sir, before you became involved in this trouble.'

'*Before I became involved*—!' Jim read strong anger into the tone of Hal Davis' harsh voice. 'I never robbed that bank an' I never shot that night watchman! I was home flat on my back sound asleep, and my mother can testify to that effect. This ain't no trial! This is a political farce. You and the judge here and these county saps hate us farmers. You're all cowmen and you hate us farmers!'

'That's right, Hal!'

'You tell 'em, Hal Davis!'

Jim hoped the trial would not end in a riot. Feeling sure was running hot and high through the farmers. But he could hardly blame them. They were all strangers, and this new land was not treating them in the manner the railroad's brochure had claimed they would be greeted. They were fighting with the only implement they had, and that implement was force.

He heard the smash of the gavel and then he heard the sheriff say, 'Deputy, you take that end of the hall. You, the other deputy, take this end. Clear this hall, savvy. Prisoner, stay where you are! If anybody pulls against you, men, shoot and shoot to kill. Now clear out, all of you!'

Jim heard muttering, but no voices were raised in high protest. He heard boots move, and men spilled out on the porch. One farmer said, 'We've got votes, Sheriff, and you won't be in your soft office settin' on your wide rump next term, believe you me.'

'We'll wait for election time,' the sheriff retorted.

Jim heard the farmers talking out on the street. They were all cursing his bank. One offered the opinion that maybe Jim had robbed his own bank and just laid the blame on the farmers. He laid his evidence down in loud tones that came through the window and were clear despite the noises made by the wind in the rafters.

From what he had heard Jim Clayton had spent a lot of money on his Willow Creek spread.

'That Bar T has some pureblooded Hereford bulls that was trailed in about a year ago from down in Wyomin'. An' them purebreds cost money an' plenty of jack, too. Then Jim owns part of the Nelson Circle S, too, although it is a little share, they tell me.'

'What about it?' a man demanded.

'*What about it*? Tuttle, you talk like a complete idjit, you do! The Circle S has some of the high-priced bulls, too. Jim might have run his bank money low payin' for them bulls. If he could lay his shortages on us farmers, he'd be plumb sure to do it, an' don't trouble your haid about that. Thet man wants us farmers out so we can't come in against his range an' the range of the Circle S. Thet Nelson gal an' him is right friendly, they is. Number of times I've seen them lolly-gaggin' out on the range. An' what right has a gal to ride out alone miles from nowhere with a man, I ask you?'

Jim hollered down, 'Shut your big mouth!'

'Who's talkin'?'

'Jim Clayton. If I was well I'd come down

and shove your big mug into the dust to silence you.'

'You're lucky you're shot up, Clayton.'

'Close your can, fellow.'

'Watch your talk or I'll come up an'—'

'Come on, fella. Hey, men, break it up. That banker can hear us. We'll talk this over in a group later on. Watch your cards and keep your lips buttoned.'

The men moved out of earshot, talking angrily as they went. Jim cursed his bum leg and his bum luck. But by now he knew one thing, and he knew it for sure. The farmers were dead set against him and his bank. This range was clearly divided into two factions: the farmers against the cowmen and the local banker. He didn't like it one bit, but what could he do about it?

He pondered his question a long while but reached no concrete answer. Maybe he had been lucky he had had a bum leg. Had he been well the judge possibly might have got him on the stand and the county attorney might have cross-questioned him, and Jim would have had to tell the truth about seeing a rider who looked like Hal Davis leaving the scene of the bank robbery.

This would have angered the farmers still more. And had he been well he might have been the unwilling center of a mob riot. And he wanted none of that. Not that he was especially afraid—he was brave enough—but he was smart enough not to want to get beaten up. And had he been able to get down to the sidewalk he would have gotten beaten up, no two ways about that. These farmers were out for blood. One of their members was indicted for murder. And *murder* is an ugly word in any language...

Then a sudden thought took hold of him. Maybe Hal Davis had not robbed the bank. Everybody seemed to have taken it for granted that Hal had been the robber, though the evidence was rather skimpy. All except the fact that the law had found Davis' wounded horse. And how did the law know for sure that the horse had been stung by a bullet? A cougar might have tried to down him and might have driven him back into the rough country. And a cougar might have clawed him across the rump. A cougar could sure tear a rip out of a bronc, as Jim knew from experience.

But if Davis had not been the robber, then who had robbed the outfit? Jim could find no answer to this. Try as he might, he could not match an answer to that question. This was a game of close checkers, and some of the plays, for some reason, were not logical. Or were they logical?

But one thing was dead certain: the farmers

now hated him more than ever. This brought his mind around to his Bar T Ranch. He would warn Jake Stone to be doubly careful. Jake was alone on the ranch. This was the dull season between spring and fall roundup and there was no use in keeping hired hands. Jake rode water-holes and shoved cattle from one section of the range to another. When Jake came in to bid him goodby, he told his foreman to be wary.

'Shucks, James, you sound like Jake Stone was a totterin' kid in diapers. I kin take care of myself.'

'Listen for those guinea hens, Jake.'

They kept guinea hens round since the trouble with the farmers had popped up its anything but gentle head. For a guinea hen has a dog beat as a watchdog. A dog will doze off, but a guinea hen never seems to sleep. They roost out away from a house either on implements like hayracks and hayloaders or in surrounding trees. In Arizona and New Mexico they used to use them instead of watchdogs to warn of Apaches and other tribes of redskins who had the grisly habits of sneaking in and wiping out ranches with death and fire. A savage can kill a dog, for the dog is on the ground, but he has a hard time killing something perched high in the air and that can fly and that never seems to sleep.

'If'n we don't git shut of them fool hens, Jim, I'll die of lack of sleep. All the night they cackle an' make that ungodly noise of theirs.'

'They're all right. You want somebody out with you for the night?'

'Sure, I'll take along that new blonde gal that is down at Ma Fallon's. Seen her on the street today. She's got a nice walk.'

'Her name is Jeff.'

'Jeff? Odd name for a girl even in her line of work.' Suddenly Jake Stone was suspicious. 'How come you all know her name?'

'Somebody told me.'

'Oh, yeah!'

An hour after Jake had left town Jim had another visitor. Belle Davis had come to pick up her satchel. She said hello and loaded her belongings—her gauze and tape and the other implements of her nursing trade. Her back was toward Jim and he was sure she kept her back to him so she would not have to speak to him. She had a nice back. She was a little the hour-glass type, but not too much so inclined. She packed her bag and snapped it shut, and then Jim spoke slowly.

'You leaving for good?'

'For good.'

'I'm a sick man.'

'You're not sick. You're well enough to offer to fight a bunch of my friends by hollering down at them from a hotel window when they stood talking.'

'Your friends, eh.'

'Yes, *my* friends!'

The implication was clear. Jim was of the town bunch—the banker-cowman herd—and she was a farmer. This line was strong and clearly defined. It stood out like a giant in a crowd of pygmies.

'Okay,' Jim said. 'Okay.'

She had her hand on the doorknob. Her face was a little strained, and Jim sensed she fought to keep her words from becoming too hard and too harsh.

'You stay with your friend Linda James. She's your kind, *banker*!'

'Linda? Wait—'

But she was gone. Her heels made savage little clicks in the hall. They stabbed the length of the hall, pivoted around the corner, then stabbed down the stairs. Jim heard the outer door of the lobby slam viciously. He did not smile. This farmer girl was plenty mad.

Oh, well, what difference does it make, Jim Clayton? Women get mad and get over it, and what diff does it make, anyway? Maybe Cyn was right; just a farmer's daughter. But a pretty farmer's daughter.

He secretly cursed his bum leg. He sat up in bed. He had pajamas over the bottom part of him, but his chest was bare. He succeeded in sitting up with an apparent effort. He had been in bed just long enough to become weak.

He felt a little giddy. The bed wanted to become a merry-go-round under him. He waited and it steadied. But he was sitting up. Blood rushed into his legs and his thigh throbbed. But there was very little pain. He sat for about five minutes and then felt stronger. He got slowly to his feet and marvelled at the strength a man can lose after a few days in bed. It took a lot of strength to even do such a simple thing as walk. Should he try to walk?

He looked at the far end of his hotel room. Before he had been shot he could have walked that distance in three strides. But now—He got on his feet, and his knees were not steady. Strength came to him. He remembered wishing he could go down on the sidewalk and tangle with the farmers. One of them could have blown his nose and knocked him off his feet. Some fight he would have put up. . .

His feet moved across the carpet. He was almost to the end of the room when a quick knock came at the door. He had been so busy with his efforts to navigate he had not heard the person's coming. First he thought it was Doc Smith coming for an evening checkup of his patient. He did not want the doctor to catch him out of bed. He hurried, as best he could, for the bed. He found the edge of it and swung under the sheet.

'Come in.'

He was sitting up when Linda James entered. He thought, This is twice she visited me today, and then he remembered she now had a room at the hotel and was just down the hall. Just trying to be a good neighbor, he thought. He was suddenly keenly aware of his undraped chest.

'I got my pants on though,' he joked.

He meant it as a joke. Evidently she did not consider it in that light. He realized he had said the wrong thing. She might deal faro and work in the midst of dancehall girls and cursing, drinking men, but she sure seemed a straight one, even though the Silver Dollar did have Ma Fallon and her girls in the back cribs.

'I came by to see how you were.' She looked at him suddenly. 'You're flushed. Have you been trying to get out of bed?'

These women! What they can't see with their eyes God lets them see with their suspicions! Can they really read the human male mind?

'No.'

She studied him in her thoughtful way. She was thin and beautiful; she was dark and lovely; God had touched her with a special wand. Yet there was a side of her that no man could ever plumb, no matter how much she loved him. Jim was aware of this. He was aware, too, of this woman's sincerity. She would make her choice, and it would be her final choice. He was sure of that. He could not tell why he was sure. But he was as sure of that as of the fact that the sun will always rise and set, there shall be a moon, that grass will grow and reclaim the earth. He was as sure of this fact as he was that some day his body would grow numb and silent under the silent touch of Death.

First, there was her slow thoughtfulness. She seemed to be weighing each word, each incident, each happening. She gave the impression that is given by a still mountain pool of water. Clear, yet you cannot see to its bottom; still, yet still moved deep underneath by unseen currents. She was not hard. She was quiet and she was deep; she was not a riddle and yet she was a riddle. Did that make sense? A riddle, and still not a riddle?

Jim said, 'I'm glad you came.'

'I thought I would look in on you, seeing your nurse had left. She was a good nurse, too, was she not?'

'She was.'

'She has a lot yet to learn.'

Jim nodded. 'Sometimes we never learn,

Miss James.'

'What do you mean by that?'

'Just . . . nothing.'

She said, 'Well, I have to go, sir. Be good and have no wild thoughts. You will do that, please?'

'Yes.'

After she had gone, after her heels had died into the distance, Jim lay on his back, his hands clasped behind his head, and thought long and hard about a slim dark-haired beauty who worked in a saloon that had an annex where certain women plied woman's long known art.

And the more he thought the less clear his thoughts became.

CHAPTER ELEVEN

The next few days were busy days for Banker Jim Clayton. Of course his bank was closed for a day or so until his bookkeeper found out to the penny how much money had been stolen. After a thorough check the stolen sum was found to be a little under thirty thousand bucks. Therefore the guess made by Ike Wilson had not been far off.

They were not easy days for Jim. Here he

was in bed and his bank was locked, and people were wondering whether or not it would open again. In fact, he was worried about that matter himself. His insurance would be a big help, but it would only pay back about twelve thousand. And that sum wasn't much cash to have in a bank. The more he thought about it the more he became convinced that Hal Davis had not robbed his bank.

Clarity and sane thinking made it hard to imagine Davis in the role of a bank robber. Whoever had looted the bank had done a professional job, and the sheriff had traced down Hal Davis' background very carefully. He came over the second day to make a personal report to Jim. The sheriff had got to the railroad and wired back East, and all he could find out from Davis' former home was that Hal had been a studious, hard-working kid who had gone religiously to Sunday school and had never been entangled before with the law.

'What do you think, Jim?'

Frankly, Jim didn't know what to think; for that matter, he didn't even know how to answer the lawman's question.

The sheriff had to return to the county seat, and he left Deputies Hank Jones and Will Lawson behind for a final checkup. They of course found nothing, and after three more days Hank Jones left. Deputy Will Lawson would stay in town until watchman Elmer Hawkins got on his feet. The old watchman was getting along as nicely as could be expected for a man his age. Doc Smith proclaimed the crisis over with and went on a drunk. With Belle Davis gone, Linda James pitched in and became a nurse. True to Doc's prophecy, Jim was on his feet within two days. He was weak and he wore a bandage, but he was almighty glad to navigate again under his own power. He would not let Linda James dress his wound, although she offered to dress it. For some reason he didn't want her to look at the hole in his thigh.

The insurance man came and went, after making his adjustment. Bank examiners came from Helena and probed the bank's books and then left. Jim got a buckboard and went to the county seat, where he borrowed ten thousand from the county bank. He then had twenty-two thousand in capital, and he reopened his bank. The few farmers that had lost money in the holdup came in and immediately withdrew their funds. Jim paid them off with a straight face.

'This dinero goes into a tin can an' gits buried,' one said loudly.

Jim said wryly, 'Don't forget where you

bury that tin can, fellow.'

The farmer looked sourly at him and went outside. Jim winked at his bookkeeper. The old man took his job ever so seriously. He was worried because the bank was in debt. Therefore he had a sour look on his dour face.

'It isn't that bad,' Jim assured him. 'We're both alive, friend.'

'This trouble sure isn't over, Jim.'

Jim had to nod at that.

His old bookkeeper had hit the nail on the head. Now the range was divided openly into two hostile camps. Previous to the bank robbery the break had been present but not so well defined. Now it was a huge deep crevice, and on one side were the farmers, hostile and impoverished and vigilant; on the other were the townspeople and the cowboys and the cowmen. The rift was deep, but it was not so wide it could not be jumped when time and anger so demanded.

When would that jump be taken?

Old Hans Nelson was for taking it immediately. He pounded the table with a gnarled, rope-calloused hand, and he cursed the farmers with fluid elasticity. He had lost dinero when the bank had been held up, and the farmer who had held it up was in jail, but there was no satisfaction in that, because Hal Davis would not reveal where he had hidden the rest of the stolen money. Old man Hawkins was so unaccommodating he would not die so a murder charge could be brought against Davis and the man would either be hanged or put away in Deer Lodge pen for life. But old Hawkins had never been a very obliging fellow anyway and was really not much account.

Jim listened and smiled. Occasionally he winked at Cyn, but on this particular day the blonde girl was not responsive, and he worried more about this than he did about Old Hans Nelson's tirade against the pumpkin-rollers. He got the impression that Cyn was fed up with this wind and this squabbling and jawing. Time was running short, and soon she would leave for Chicago.

Strangely, he did not hate to see her go. He tried to find the reason for that lack of emotion but could not lay his thumb on its source. He felt swell physically. His leg had healed, and he could ride a bronc, he could walk and run. Mentally he was not so well. This trouble was always in the back of his mind, seeking a solution that seemed impossible to find. It was a shifting, silent mirage; it moved in and tantalized him: it darted and shifted aside, and it left nothing but a gnawing unrest.

'I'll tell old Hawkins he should be obliging

and he should die, Old Hans.'

'You both talk like a couple of idiots!' Cyn was unusually sharp.

Mrs. Nelson looked up from her knitting. 'Tell the fools that again, Cyn!' Her eyes went back to her work.

'You two women shut up!' Old Hans was angry.

Cyn winked at her mother. 'The boss just gave an order, Mother.'

Old Hans spoke to Jim. 'Me, I figure mebbe ol' Hawkins ain't so dumb, Jim. Fact is, he might've identified thet bandit but won't reveal his name 'cause he might aim to handle him personally when he gits well. He's a stubborn, proud ol' coot, Hawkins is.'

Jim had been nursing this same thought, but he just nodded absently. He felt sure that with Mrs. Nelson and Cyn holding a tight rein on Old Hans, the old cowman would not move against the farmers in open warfare. Old Hans might talk and holler, but those two women folks had a tough jawstrap on him. Jim was glad of that. Old Hans might lose his head and his temper and get killed.

As for old man Hawkins . . . Old Hans had really said something. Hawkins would take no money from his children, would accept no county aid—he was, in fact, very proud. He was the type who would nurse something until the time was ripe and then he would hit.

Jim went to the door. This range, he decided, was too quiet. He decided, then and there, he would get off the fence, if he had ever been on one. From now on it was either Jim Clayton or the farmers. They hated him; he knew that. He did not hate them. But he had to protect himself.

He said goodby, tried to catch Cyn's glance; he failed in this and rode from the Circle S yard with his bronc at a walk and feeling rather dour. He headed for his Bar T outfit on Willow Creek. Dust and more dust and the hot stillness of a late afternoon in late August. After Cyn left he doubted if he would ever see much of her again.

Cyn wanted to marry and have a home and children. He knew that, for she had told him so. She wasn't going to college to get a graduate degree; she was going to look for a good man.

For some reason he realized she was doing what was evidently the best thing in her case. He would lose her, he knew. This did not especially hurt him. When she was at a distance she was just like a sister; when she got close she was a sweetheart. That was an odd way for him to think. Yet it was the truth. Now he didn't think that way about Belle Davis.

He swung his bronc, rode over the hill, and came down on the Davis ranch. When he rode around the barn he saw two broncs tied to the hitching post in front of the spread. He recognized them as belonging to Dan Shepard and Ike Wilson. These two, he decided, were very close friends. He wished he had not fallen victim to his sudden desire to see the girl again. Had it been possible he would have ridden on but it was too late, for they had seen him turn into the ranch. And Dan Shepard, blast his black soul, wasn't putting Jim Clayton to flight!

When he pulled in his sorrel Belle and Dan Shepard came from the house. Belle had been laughing, but when she saw him her laughter left her. She asked coldly, 'What do you want, banker?'

'A drink of water,' Jim said.

Shepard said, 'There's water in the creek.'

'You drink it, fellow.'

Ike Wilson came out of the house, and his boots made solid sounds across the floor of the porch. 'Is there trouble out here?' He asked the world in general. Behind him peered Mrs. Davis.

Jim thought, I sure made a mistake when I rode down here.

'No trouble,' Jim said.

'I think there is.' Wilson was a bulldog. He

wanted to get his teeth into this and tug and tear. The heavy insult in the man's thick voice rasped like a dull wood-file against Jim's usual good nature. Had the farmer been in town Jim would have tied into him, but there were two women present and Jim was on private property. So he made to turn his horse, and as he reined him around he looked at Belle. Her face was high with color. She didn't seem to be as angry as her first words had hinted. Jim caught this impression, tasted of it, and found it good for some reason.

'Good day, folks.'

Wilson reached out and caught Jim's reins, and the banker's bronc stopped. Jim sat saddle and felt a wryness in him. He knew that if he ever got on the ground both the land-locator and the farmer would tie into him and beat the stuffing out of him. He knew that as sure as his bronc had four hoofs. He had to get out of here and he had to do it fast.

'Let go my reins!'

'Get off that bronc!'

The rest was action—swift and sure and planned. Mrs. Davis cried, 'Please, men, no fighting,' and Belle said, 'Watch your words and actions and no fighting here—' But Jim was acting. His right boot came out. It smashed against Ike Wilson's heavy neck and kicked back his Adam's apple. Wilson gulped something and went back under the impact. His fingers lost their grip and he fell in the dust. He rolled over and clutched his throat. He could not speak. He just gasped and sputtered. He was very sick; Jim could not have kicked him in a better place. Jim had his .45 out, and it covered land-locator Dan Shepard.

'Lift your hands, mister. There, that's better. Belle, get Wilson's gun, please.'

'I won't do it.' Stubbornly.

'Then your damned stubborn pride demands that you see a man—or some men—get killed?'

The impact was plain. Her tongue came out; she wet her lips. Yet pride clung and anger was with her and these showed. Wilson sat up and held his throat and did not look at Jim, for pain was with him. And Dan Shepard stood with his hands high and that sad sick look on his lean face. He was immaculate and his tie was just right, and the diamond stickpin made facets of light. He just stood there and was silent, and his face was very sad.

'Get their guns!'

Mrs. Davis spoke sternly, and Jim sent her a glance. She was fully aware of the danger in this, and this showed on her pain-filled old face. She hobbled forward, the pain strong in her, and then her daughter pulled back. Belle took Shepard's gun and she got the Colt from Wilson.

Jim said, 'Give them to me.'

She hesitated. She looked at Dan Shepard. Shepard said quietly, 'Give the little boy the big bad guns.' He could joke. Apparently this was not serious to him. But Jim knew the joking was just a front.

She handed Jim the guns one at a time. He stuck them in his belt, and then his own weapon went down and found its leather. He said, 'Water will do them good,' and he gave them all a quick glance. Mrs. Davis was standing with her cane, and her eyes showed their ever-present pain; her daughter was God's own, and she showed this; Wilson was sitting and he was silent. For a moment Jim's eyes met those of Wilson's. What he read there made him a little sick in his belly. Then he looked at the lonesome face of land-locator Dan Shepard.

'Shepard, you're behind all this trouble, man. Do you sleep good at nights?'

'Do you?'

Put a question aginst a question... An old form of avoiding an issue. Jim had used it in debate at the university. There was nothing here but uncertainty and hate, and both were rotten for the soul. So Jim Clayton pranced his bronc sideways out of the yard. He was taking no chances. They hated him—these two men did—and maybe there was a rifle in the house. They could run for it and bring it up and he would come out of saddle and he would be dead. This trouble had reached such a terrible stage. Nothing could stop it now except letting Death take his toll. Jim was sure of that and doubly sure. So he cakewalked his saddler out of the yard, and this way he watched them. When he went past the water trough his free arm made a movement and the guns slid in with a slight splash. Wet them down, water and kill their strength. Water is what this land needs. We are fighting over water. Laugh, water, laugh, for we are just silly mortals.

He came to the hill, and then he turned the horse almost savagely; he lifted him and used his rowels and the pony ran with his belly level. The hill rose behind him and the farm was gone. Jim rode twisted in stirrups, letting the pony travel; he had his reins looped around the saddle-horn. He had his short-gun raised, and he caught the smell of the barrel, and it still smelled of burned powder. This was an acrid smell, faint though it was to his nostrils; it did not smell good. For it was the smell of evil. The man who made the first gun made all men the same size. Yes, and he made all men miserable. But if he had not invented it, some other man would have. Jim was thinking of this, and the thought was alien. It did not fit the present situation.

But other thoughts did. Now where did he stand with Belle? He remembered drifting down that hill, his pony running wild, and he remembered the team and buckboard below him, bouncing in run-away wildness. The wind had touched her and the gods had been good; the wind had shown her roundness, and her face had been sweet. Now it was not sweet. It was against him; that hurt him.

Goodby, Belle, he thought.

No! That was not right! A young man is a young man and he has his dreams, and those dreams clash with reality. The wind can sing through the pines and the wind is good; the wind does not change except in velocity—its texture is always the same. Only man and woman change. The touch of fingers, the movement of lips, then reality comes in. Jim thought, I'll wait and see.

He remembered Wilson sitting there and grabbing at his throat. Then the pain had fallen back and anger had pushed to the front. Wilson had sat there, and his eyes and his mouth had told their harsh story. Wilson had a very low intelligence. He owned his own stubborn pride. He had lost face and he would fight to regain it. He was Jim's deadly enemy.

Jim realized that, and yet it held no fear. He

thought of Dan Shepard. How could a man have the soft eyes of a doe and be hard as a horned buck? That did not make good logic, it was not natural. Yet it was true. Shepard was his enemy, but Shepard would not act now. He had Wilson, and Wilson had reached fever pitch; Shepard was going to use Wilson. Shepard was that type. Use the other man, take advantage of him, employ him. Let him fight your battles. Dumb, stupid fool, feed his vanity, personal vanity; you use him indirectly. Use him like a puppet. Pull the mental strings, get him thinking just right; the physical movements will come. So Jim realized Ike Wilson was the one to watch for sign of open action.

He pulled his thoughts away from the scene at the Davis ranch. When he rode into his Bar T the guinea hens ran and made their noises. Jake Stone came out of the brush—wide, tough Jake; faithful Jake—and Jake looked at him.

'You've had trouble,' Jake said. 'Tell Unc about it, Jim.'

Jim told about the fight with Wilson. Jake fingered the rifle. 'I thought I heard a snooper last night. I combed the brush but found nothin'. Well, Wilson is out for you, little boy.'

'Let him come!'

CHAPTER TWELVE

On his ride back to Valley Center Jim mulled over the fact that Jake Stone had claimed he had heard a snooper in the brush. Although Jake had found nobody there still was a chance that a snooper had been scouting the Bar T. The farmers hated him and he figured some of them wouldn't be too high and mighty to burn down his cow outfit.

And Jake was level-headed. He wasn't one to go off on a wild tangent and hear imagined noises.

Two miles from his ranch he met a surprise. For Belle Davis came riding toward him. She held her right hand high in the Sioux sign of peace, and Jim pulled in and awaited her. His smile hid his surprise ... or so he hoped.

'Figured you'd scalp me the next time you saw me, Belle.'

She smiled, and her smile was sweet. 'Oh, I wasn't mad at you long, Jim. I came over to apologize for Mother and me. I'm sorry I acted the way I did. Really, neither of those two—either Shepard or Wilson—mean anything to me. Just acquaintances, nothing more.'

Jim thought, Yeah, just acquaintances. And

the other day I saw you kissing Shepard back in the alley behind his office. You didn't see me because I was looking out an upstairs window in the Town Hotel. He said, 'Apologies accepted, Miss Belle. And I offer mine for my conduct. Reckon I just lost my temper.'

'You had a reason.'

Their horses fell in side by side. Jim sent a covert glance at the girl. Her face was pensive, almost fragile; she seemed to be deep in thought. Jim found himself wondering if she were the angel she acted. She was a pretty deep subject. He decided to have some fun.

'Belle.'

'Yes.'

She stopped her horse. He stopped his. Her eyes were expectant. Jim's horse moved in and his arm went around her. She was limp and soft and he had his ideas. Her face raised.

'Why, Jim . . .'

Her lips never closed completely. He saw to that. Her lips clung and were moist, and she knew how. Jim found that he was the one to break. Her eyes were closed. Did she keep them closed to hide her thoughts?

Jim said, 'You're changeable, Belle.'

Her eyes opened. Her gaze was steady and soft. 'That's a woman's right . . . so they tell me.'

'What's your game?'

Still that soft-as-silk look. Still those big eyes traveling across his face. Still the lips opened slightly.

'I don't understand you, Jim.'

'You're after something.'

The look left. Her eyes became opaque. Her lips became closed. When she spoke they seemed thinner. They barely moved.

'Jim, you hurt me. Maybe I love you, Jim.'

Jim shook his head. 'I don't think so. In fact, I know you don't. I got a hunch you love nobody but Belle Davis.' Cruel words, but sometimes you have to be cruel. You beat metal with a big sledge to test its qualities. Words do the same to some humans.

'You don't know a thing, Jim Clayton!'

She turned her horse abruptly and rode away at a lope. Jim headed out after her and they swept around the base of a hill. But his bronc was tired and her horse was fresh and she rode away from him. He pulled in, stirrup leathers rising and falling as his horse gulped for air, and his smile was mystified. He put back his hat and rubbed his hair and said, 'Well, now what the devil, anyway?'

And he couldn't answer his own question.

He had other questions, also. Why had she ridden out to meet him? Surely she had had a motive for the ride? And when he had kissed her she had responded of her own free will. . . About two hours ago she had wanted to kill him, judging from her talk and her looks.

Maybe he should not have baited her. If he had played along with her he might have made a big advance. But was such an advance worth while? He figured she was trying to get on his good side so he could aid her brother. But he didn't have long to wrestle with these thoughts, for he soon saw a rider ahead of him, and the pinto told him Cynthia Nelson was heading for town. So he lifted his own horse to a lope and caught her.

'Hello, Cyn.'

'Hello, Jim.'

'Coming into town to see me?'

'You sound too confident. I'm riding in for the mail.'

She didn't seem very gay. Her face still held that serious look he had seen at the Circle S. Dust rose, and they rode through a devil-twist of it. He put his head down, and she held her handkerchief over her nose. When the dust fell apart he looked at her. She spat like a man and cursed the dust.

'I'll be glad to get out of here. Damn these farmers anyway! You can have the farmer's daughter if you want her.'

'I'd rather have you.'

'You won't get me.'

It sounded like banter, but it had a deep undercurrent in it. Jim noted this and did not feel too good. These women were giving him a rough time. But all women always gave him a bad time. They seemed to be born with that ability.

'Hope you have a good winter.'

'Well, one thing is certain: I won't buck these Montana snowdrifts with a sagebrush Romeo.' Her free hand found his wrist. 'Oh, Jim, sometimes I talk like an utter idiot. But look what this country does to its women!' She answered her own statement. 'Look at Mother! Old before her time, lines in her face, crow's feet put there by this wind. It bends you and breaks you. Finally the wind drives you howling mad.' She was very sober suddenly. 'Not for this chicken.'

Jim said, 'I like it here. That may seem odd, but I do like it here. Maybe I'm loco, but I do.'

She said, 'Two riders over yonder.' She stood on her stirrups and looked. The riders were about half a mile away and they were drifting toward town at a fast lope. 'Looks to me like his Nibs, the honorable Dan Shepard, and his stinking satellite, Ike Wilson.'

Jim said, 'That's them.'

'Now I wonder what they're up to?'

He had no answer to this. He did not tell

her about his run-in with the pair in the yard of the Davis farm. First, she'd want all the details, just like all women; then she'd start to ask questions. What was he doing over at the Davis farm? Had he ridden over to see Belle?

He wanted none of that. He was upset enough as it was. So he merely shrugged in what he hoped was a casual brush-off of the pair. As it was, Shepard and Wilson rode into Valley Center ahead of them by a mile. The pair unsaddled and put their sweaty horses into the small barn behind the land-locator's office.

'Mebbe I should go see Doc Smith?' Wilson asked.

Shepard played ignorant. 'See Doc Smith about what?'

'My throat, of course.'

'You mean you want Doc to dig the banker's toe out of it, eh?'

Wilson gave Shepard a hard look. He swung his saddle over the saddle-rack and spread out the Navaho blanket to dry.

'You sure ain't funny, Dan.'

Shepard's voice was low. He seemed to be talking directly to his horse, for he did not look at his *segundo*.

'Look, fellow, you're a tough egg, savvy? Who's told me that? Nobody but one gent named Ike Wilson. But it seems to me that a fellow named Jim Clayton kind of run over you a while back?'

'Don't rib me, Dan. I'll get Clayton, I will, I'll kill him as sure as I'm over three feet high!'

'That might be a good thing,' Shepard said.

They walked into Shepard's office by the rear door. Jeff, the new girl at Ma Fallon's place, was walking by. She saw them and knocked on the window. 'When you two comin' down again?'

'Tomorrow,' Shepard said.

Ike Wilson winked grossly at the harpy. Jeff winked back unashamedly and then continued down the street. Wilson slid close to the glass and watched her walk away until she was out of sight in his narrow field of vision. He wet his thick lips and his sore Adam's apple took a second seat.

'She's a nice filly.'

'Another one,' Dan Shepard said. He was sad again. Muggins came in and looked at him and walked close, and Shepard reached down for him. Muggins made a pass at him and walked over and rubbed against Ike Wilson's legs. His purring made a smooth sound. Shepard frowned and Wilson saw this.

'That cat don't like you, Dan.'

'No news to me. And I feed him good, too.'

'He bites the hand that feeds him, eh? My

wife was that way. She shore was an ungrateful heifer, that woman.'

Dan Shepard had already heard too much about Ike Wilson's divorced wife. He had heard so much about her that, although he had never seen her, he felt sure he would instinctively know her if and when he happened to meet her, which was a remote possibility. She evidently had been a woman of many physical charms and every facet of her character had been thoroughly gone over by her ex-husband. So Dan Shepard amused himself by watching Banker Jim Clayton ride into town with the golden-haired daughter of Old Hans Nelson.

'There's a pretty filly, too, boss.'

'That she is,' Shepard agreed.

Wilson said, 'Time I got some chuck and lighted out to my farm. I shouldn't be seen too much with you, Dan.'

'I'm a bad boy,' Shepard said.

Wilson grinned, nodded, left. Shepard watched him go up the street to the Broken Horn Café. Linda James came out of the Town Hotel and passed his office as she went to the Silver Dollar. Shepard watched her quick walk, the saucy pert set of her small head. He liked small women. And this one was a neat bundle. But he had made his play and got exactly nowhere, and she had told him to lay off in no uncertain terms. Now she passed his window. Their eyes met for a moment, and she nodded and he nodded. Each understood the other. Was she really in love with that banker? He hoped not. Some people had all the luck.

The wind blew dust. Dust ... dust ... dust. The world was made of dust. The Ohio River rolled, and the soil was wet; rain tumbled over the hills of West Virginia. Grass rolled across Kentucky hills. Colorado's foothills were dotted with cattle and grass was to their knees. Wicked cattle with long horns. Swinging those horns. And here there was dust.

Dust, dust, dust.

Sometimes you think about a certain project or plan for so long that it magnifies itself to a great size in your mind. Dan Shepard realized he had to back up and take a new look at this; his perspective was going cockeyed. Things had come out to his satisfaction. Hal Davis owned a nice piece of land, and now it was his, for that afternoon he had taken a mortgage on the Davis farm. First mortgage, too. Davis was in jail and couldn't get bail. That is, he couldn't get bail until the old watchman was out of danger completely.

He had won his point. He and Ike Wilson had the dinero from Jim Clayton's bank. The sheriff had given up searching for any other clues, for all clues pointed securely to Hal Davis. And Davis was behind bars... They had the money, and the farmers were hopping mad at Jim Clayton. Clayton was a cowman and Old Hans Nelson was a cowman, and the farmers hated them both. Now to get Old Hans or Jim Clayton to make a move. He got to his feet.

He walked the floor. His boots, polished, clean, made their sounds. His suit was neatly pressed, his silk shirt was clean and immaculate, his tie was just right. He raised his hands and looked at them. Fine hands, long hands, with clean, well-kept fingernails. No physical work showing in those soft hands. They were the hands of a man who lived by his brain.

He walked. He put his hands behind him. He stopped. He took his hands and folded them and stood still. He had it. The farmers hated Clayton—some even accused him of robbing his own bank—but Clayton had paid off his depositors and had taken the loss himself. When Clayton had paid off the few farmers who had had money in his bank, some of the hate had melted.

Well, he'd get Clayton to hate the farmers. He had worked the farmers to the limit against Clayton. Now he would work Clayton against the farmers.

His face became very calm. Muggins looked at him from the seat where he sat with his front paws folded under him. Shepard started toward the cat, rage in his eyes; then he stopped.

Muggins watched him. His eyes were wide. He did not purr.

Dan Shepard watched the tomcat. Dan Shepard said, 'What the dickens? He's just a cat, the thing is. Just a cat.'

They eyed each other.

Now Dan Shepard's eyes were sad.

Muggins' eyes were yellow. They were wary.

Shepard got his hat and walked outside. Muggins watched him until the door was closed.

Muggins closed his eyes and slept.

CHAPTER THIRTEEN

For four days peace seemed to have come to Valley Center range. Of course Old Hans Nelson growled like a love-sick bobcat and made dire threats toward the farmers, and of course his wife and daughter held him back. Cyn packed for her trip East and knew the deepest of misgivings. She got the idea that she was running away just when her parents needed her the most, and she told this to her mother who vehemently opposed this theory. The girl did not know whether to go or stay home. Her mother wanted her to go. She knew very well the unrest, the loneliness, her daughter experienced. She had no close good friends, and young men were scarce. She would have liked to have seen Cyn and Jim get married. But she was never one to push her desires onto somebody else, be they kin or just friends. She figured that Cynthia would tire of Chicago and come home, and maybe then she and Jim would marry. She was content to bide her time. Fate and Time had a way of accomplishing many things.

The farmers stood night-guard and discussed the situation over their barbwire fences, and now and then they looked toward a cloudless sky as though to plea for rain which never came.

Dust grew thicker, if that were possible.

The water level fell in wells. Pot-holes took the place of creeks, and springs that never before had gone dry now dried up. Out on the open range Bar T and Circle S cattle had to go further and further for water. Grass was so thin they would graze out one day and graze back toward water the second day. They trekked through the sagebrush and greasewood, patient and walking in lines, and their ribs showed. Beef profits would be small.

Wolves drifted down from Canada. Jim found one of his purebred Hereford bulls dead beside Wishing Springs. Wolves had killed the valuable animal. They had torn into his carcass. Jim set traps but caught nothing but a coyote. The wolves were too wise to step into traps, however well camouflaged.

More farmers hit Jim for loans which they did not get. This increased their antipathy toward him and the bank. They tried to get money from Dan Shepard, but Shepard professed financial collapse. The railroad was even debating, he said, about whether or not to turn north at Spur Junction and go over to Lewistown; they might not even lay rails into Valley Center. This scared the farmers very much. Without a railroad they could not ship out crops ... if they had any crops. And the next year might be a wet year with lots of wheat. But a hard winter with cold weather and lots of snow would wipe them out. The Sioux said it would be a hard winter with very little snow, though. And no snow meant no spring moisture.

Jake Stone kept up a constant guard at Jim's Bar T ranch. One word fitted faithful

Jake; that word was *loyal*. Some men are that way. Financially and socially they cut no great figures, so they attach themselves to some man, usually a younger man, and they work with him and he becomes their god as he goes up the ladder. Jake was that way toward Jim.

Linda James hung on at the Silver Dollar, even though the proprietor threatened to close the dive because of lack of trade. Ma Fallon talked more strongly about taking her girls and moving on to the Little Rocky gold fields.

The girl named Jeff left town one afternoon, boarding the stage with great howdeedoo. She made a scowl fit Ike Wilson's ugly mug. Ike talked with a guttural note, and they wondered what had happened to his voice. Two days later Jeff returned. She was dusty and tired. Zortman and Landusky, she reported, were filled with errant females. A girl couldn't make an honest buck there. She winked at Jim Clayton who winked back. She had a slow, tantalizing, come-hither wink. Ike Wilson saw them wink, but he bided his time. He glowered at Jim, who smiled back. Ike waited for the time and the place.

Jeff went back to work on commission at Ma Fallon's house.

Unbeknown to Jim, the wink had also been noticed by Linda James. But if it bothered Linda one bit, her thin dark face gave no hint of a disturbance. She walked toward the hotel.

'Hello, Jim.'

'Hello, Miss James.'

She showed him a dark smile, and her eyes were dark. 'Linda, please; not Miss James.'

'Linda, then.'

'That's better.'

'Things are quiet,' Jim said.

'Very quiet.'

But that night the tempo suddenly increased. A rider came in from the county seat on a bronc that was white with lather and wobbly in his knees from the hard ride in the heat of sundown. Hal Davis had broken jail. Men and women and kids crowded around him, and dogs barked in excitement. Harley Brown's jackass even started to bray, but he did that each sundown. Widder Hopkins said he was lonely for another jackass.

'How'd he break out? With a gun?'

'No, with a spoon.'

'A—a what—?'

People stared at each other and then stared at the messenger.

'Come again, sir,' the deputy said slowly and in surprise.

The man then told the entire story. He was a master of suspense and he talked slowly. People became anxious, but the man continued on in the same dead tone of voice.

Jim listened and waited. Linda James moved close to him and looked up and smiled. Then Linda looked back at the man on horseback.

The story was very simple. Hal Davis had kept back a spoon from a tray of grub handed to him by the jailer. The jailer had not missed the spoon. Hal had twisted it into a key and had sprung the lock and had walked out past the jailer when he had been taking his evening siesta. He had got a gun and gunbelt and some cartridges, and he also had got a Winchester .30-30 from the rack.

'He done even stole the sheriff's top bronc, he did.'

'Good,' a farmer said emphatically. He was a gross man, wide and heavy; he looked around belligerently. His gaze met the eyes of Jim and Jim looked away. The farmer wanted trouble, and Jim did not want to please him. He walked toward his bank slowly. Linda James fell into step beside him.

'Is it possible, Jim, that a man could twist a spoon into a key and break jail? That seems improbable to me.'

Jim admitted it seemed improbable to him, also. But things had happened so fast and the pace had been so furious the last few months he allowed that anything could be possible.

'I'm even beginning to doubt if I am really alive.'

'Oh, you're alive all right, even though your eyes are closed most of the time.' She smiled, and this took the sting from her words.

He smiled, too.

He found that he smiled easily when around Linda. When with Belle Davis he was always on guard, almost searching for the correct words; with Cyn he had to be sharp and alert, for Cynthia was not slow herself. But with Linda it was different. With Linda, for some odd reason, he felt at home. They thought in the same direction and had the same thoughts about many things. Either that or she was deliberately bending her way to match his. She was smart enough. He found himself wondering how old she was and where she had been born and who her parents were and how she became a gambler.

'How old are you?'

'Why, Jim, the sudden change of pace, man! What difference does it make?'

'I wouldn't marry a woman older than I was.'

Her laugh was smooth. It was like old wine moving from one glass to another. 'Maybe I should first ask how old you are and then I'd be sure to be younger than you. But I won't. I'm twenty-three.'

'When's your birthday?'

'Gosh, you are really ambitious, aren't you

now? Maybe you do intend to marry me. Well, sir, I'll be twenty-four next March twenty-second. Now am I younger or older than you?'

'I'll be twenty-four on March twentieth.'

'I win by two days.'

'Where were you born?'

They were in front of his bank. She stopped and looked up at him. Her head was tilted; he wished it were not so dark. He would have liked to have seen her eyes. Were they serious or saucy?

'Are you a lawyer cross-examining me?'

'Yes, I am.'

'I was born, sir, in Old Mexico. In Sonora State, sir. I went to convent school—oh, how I hated it! I liked to study, but I hated confinement. I saw my mother occasionally: she was a grand lady with grand clothing—the sweetest perfume. When I was sixteen I ran away. I found out then that my mother was a gambler. I fell in love with gambling, and here I am.'

'Your father?'

Her lips pursed. 'You know, I cannot remember a father in my life. Once I asked Mother, and she hushed me up and I never asked again. My mother is in New Orleans now, dealing faro.'

'And how did you come to this section of

Montana, fair lady?'

'More questions... I came because I got sick of the city. And rotten men that figured just because a woman was a gambler she could not be a lady.'

'Do you like it here?'

'Jim, I love it!'

He caught the edge of her enthusiasm and thought. She loves this land, and Cyn was raised here and she hates it. It didn't make sense. It was like life and many other things.

'The wind, Jim, and cattle on the hills. Sure, I know the drouth is here, but it will go, and grass will come back and cattle will be fat. Jim, I want to die on a cow ranch. I've found where I want to be. I've found what I've searched for.'

Jim felt a little taken back by her sincerity. He caught a glimpse of her character and found it deep and satisfying.

'I like it here, too.'

She was thoughtful, and her voice showed her concern. 'These poor farmers. They believe everything that Shepard tells them. Some know that Shepard is working them, I believe.'

'It should be apparent by now.' Jim unlocked his bank, for he had some night work to do. 'But sometimes a man can't see things that are too close to him.'

'I've noticed that.'

Now what the heck did she mean by that? She was turning back to womanhood's old standby; talk in riddles.

'Well me for supper, then to work. Goodby, Jim.'

'Goodby.'

Jim went into the bank and locked the door behind him. The place had the same odors: rather close in atmosphere, the smell of ink and ledgers and day books, the scent of floor oil. Long habit made him cross the lobby without hitting a chair or desk and brought him to the lamp which he lit and carried back to his room. He had some desk work to finish.

So Hal Davis had broken out of the county jail... The silly fool! He had only made the evidence against him, slight though it was, loom larger. When he had picked the door lock with a spoon he had further strengthened the theory that he had also picked the door to the bank's vault. Up to now people had claimed he had not been able to pick the bank's vault-lock. Now they were saying different. Jim had heard that talk pass through the crowd.

'If he could've opened that jail-house door with a spoon, then it must have been child's play for him to pick the safe dial.'

Justice of Peace Ed Winchester had been

the speaker. Now Jim Clayton thumped a pencil up and down on his desk and gave this matter deep thought. Yet despite the gravity of his thoughts, the memory of Linda James kept creeping to the front. He put her image back and it sneaked out again. Only by sheer will-power did he force her to take a back seat.

After breaking out of jail, where did Hal Davis go? According to the messenger, the sheriff had headed out with a posse. Jim figured the sheriff would set up a watch over the Davis ranch in hopes Hal would try to contact his mother or sister, which was very probable. Again he felt sorry for Mrs. Davis. As for Belle—well, she was young and healthy and perfectly able to take care of herself. But it was different with an ailing old woman.

Jim tried to put himself in Davis' boots. The young granger would be angry and mad at the entire world. He had sure done a foolish thing by breaking out of jail. Would Davis try to make contact with Dan Shepard?

He realized Davis might be out to get him, too. Sometimes he did not pack a gun, and he decided now always to go armed. Davis had no use for him. First he had knocked the man down and then Davis had been accused of robbing his bank. Jim couldn't work on his books. He shut them and blew out the lamp and went outside. Dusk was changing into night, and the air was cooling, and it smelled good. A dog barked on the edge of town. The wind moved the cottonwoods and rustled their dusty leaves. Jim decided to go and see old man Hawkins.

Hawkins was sitting up in bed. The lamplight showed his thin, peaked face with its thick iron-grey whiskers.

'Howdy, button.'

'Hello, Elmer.'

Hawkins said, 'I was keepin' my name a secret. That sure is some handle, eh? You don't reckon my mother had a grudge against me, too?'

'I don't see why not.'

Hawkins grinned. He had better color in his face, Jim realized, although it was difficult to see his face because of his whiskers and the dimness of the kerosene lamp. But it was plain that the watchman was on the road to recovery. Jim figured the man must have been made of whale-bone and rawhide to stand the shock and smash of a slug at his advanced age.

Hawkins had not heard about Hal Davis breaking jail. This made him rather angry. 'Since thet Davis girl quit nursin' me nobody comes to see 'cept that saloon girl, Linda James, an' she comes right seldom. So he busted outa the clink... Jimmer boy, I'd walk light, was I you, an' keep out of dark alleys.'

'He hates me. No two ways about that.'

'He was a fool. He had no call to jump jail. A trial this fall would have cleared him.'

'How do you know?'

Jim wondered if he had not caught the oldster off-guard. But if he had, Hawkins was quick to come to his defense. What evidence did they have against Davis? Very flimsy, and evidence the court would throw out because it was all circumstantial. Hawkins had a sharp brain and he enumerated the points of evidence, discarding them as he disqualified each one. And Jim had to agree with the old watchman. Finally he reached the grudging realization that maybe Hawkins' statement had been only normal and logical.

'Wish you could have identified that bank robber, Elmer.'

He watched the man closely.

'Wish, I could've, too; but I didn't, so thet is thet.'

The old man's face looked normal, Jim realized. He got to his feet, and for some reason he felt a little baffled. This was a merry-go-round, and around and around it went, and he never could even see the brass ring, let along hook it. Somewhere in the night was Hal Davis, and Davis might be heading back to look him up, for Davis hated him. Davis was desperate. He would have a gun, and the slightest bad move, the tiniest shadow of doubt, would make him reach for that trigger. Jim decided that if Davis did look him up and jump him he would shoot first and shoot to kill. The idea was not pleasant. For one thing, it isn't a nice thing to have to kill a man, for the man who did the killing has to live with that thought; then, too, there were Belle and her mother—her crippled, sick mother.

'Watch your backtrail, button.'

'I'll do that.'

He had spent more time with Hawkins than he had thought. For when he came out in the lobby of the hotel, the night was dark. For a moment the lamps in the lobby silhouetted him, and Hawkins' warning came back and prompted him to move into the dark. There was one man on the street, and he moved slowly through the darkness. It was too dark for Jim to identify him. He went through the rectangle of light from the saloon, and he still walked bent over and his head was down. Jim thought, A drunk, and let it go at that. The man came to the bank. He sagged ahead and rammed into the door. He sat down and he pounded on the door and he called, 'Jim, oh, Jim. This is Jake.'

Jim ran toward him. When he got there

Jake Stone was lying down. Jake said, 'I got shot. A man—in the brush—the guinea hens warned me, Jim. Those hens are good watch dogs. But a hen can't be a dog, can she?'

'Quit your joshing. Who shot you and how bad?'

Jake didn't know who had shot him. He had got in some lead himself. He was hit in the chest. Already they had a crowd, and a man went after Doc Smith, who was still drunk.

'Jake, Hal Davis busted jail. Did Hal shoot you?'

'He was stocky, like Hal. Seen him from a distance, but it was too far to recognize him. God, I'm sick, Jim. Oh, it might've been Hal; but it might not have been, too. Where's that doc? He still drunk?'

'He's still drunk,' a man said.

Another said, 'Here he comes. He kin hardly navigate.'

CHAPTER FOURTEEN

They got Jake Stone into Doc Smith's office. The heavy-set medico washed his hands, belched, and almost fell down. Jim got a bucket of cold water from the pump behind in the alley. Jim was sick at heart. He seemed to be standing on the edge of a big canyon, and he wanted to fall in but he couldn't make the leap. Had Davis broke jail and headed for the Willow Creek ranch to burn it down? He wanted to get his bronc and head out for his Bar T spread, but he had to stay to see how badly Jake was wounded. Jake meant more than lumber and property.

He should have been angry; he wasn't. He felt more digusted. He got the bucket of cold water and went into the office with the water lapping behind him. He came in behind the drunken doctor. He said, 'Doc, turn around,' and when Smith turned, he met a cascade of water. Water smashed into his face and filled his mouth, and he gasped and spat. Water ran down his gravy-stained old vest. Doc Smith went to his knees and spat and spewed, and he looked up and said, 'That's one way to sober a man, Jim.'

'Get on your feet, please, and get to work.'

Deputy Will Lawson cleared the office. Only Doc Smith and Jim and the deputy and the wounded man remained in the close room. Jim opened a window, and the babble of voices from the street outside came into the room. Deputy Lawson said, 'I ride for your spread, Jim.'

Jim said, 'Just a minute, Will, and I ride with you. First I want to see how Jake is.'

'The night is dark,' Lawson said. 'We couldn't pick up track. I'll wait.' He was a massive man, and patience was a part of him. When he went after a man or an idea, he got what he wanted. His statement was correct. Darkness had rushed down and laid its black cloak across the sagebrush and greasewood and the timber and foothills. Darkness kissed the mountain tops and fondled the buffalo grass that was brown and sparse and dead.

Jake Stone opened his eyes. 'Whoever he was he might have burned the spread, Jim.'

'It would be burned down by now.'

Some of the town's kids had run to climb Mount Rocky—a high hill on the south of town—and Jim was waiting for them to return. From this point they would be able to see flames at his place. But he did not have to wait for the report from the youngsters. Within a few minutes the Wishing Rock farmer, Jack Haynes, came into town at a lope.

'Fire out along Willow Crick, men. Flames high in the air. Looks to me like Pete Sawyer's farm is on fire.'

Somebody said, 'Must be Jim's ranch.'

'You mean the banker's outfit. Wahl, now, that is logical. Hope it burns plumb to the foundation. Wonder who set it?'

Jim heard the farmer's cutting words.

When somebody told Jack Haynes that Jake Stone had been shot, Haynes laughed a little. It was a low laugh, a mean laugh; Jim looked at Jake, who lay with his eyes closed. Jake Stone's face was without blood. Jim walked outside.

Doc Smith glanced at him, but said nothing.

Jim said, 'Let me through,' and a man moved. A ripple moved ahead, too: it said, 'Jim Clayton's coming, Haynes.' Haynes moved his bronc, and Jim grabbed the reins. Jim said, 'Get off that horse, farmer!'

'I won't do it! I want no trouble!'

'You talked big. Now back up your words. You or one of your scissorbills lit my spread on fire. One of you shot my partner.'

'Weren't me, Clayton! Clayton, watch—'

Jim leaped on the horse and dragged Haynes from saddle. Forgotten was the pain in his wounded leg. Haynes packed no shortpistol, but he had a Winchester in his saddle scabbard, and he clawed at this as he went down under Jim's weight. But to get the rifle out of the boot one had to lift up, not down; Haynes was falling and therefore he could not snag the rifle.

They hit the ground and somebody jerked Haynes' bronc to one side to get him out of the way. Jim heard people holler and then he hit

Haynes. But Haynes had hit him first. A mauling blow, more luck than science; Jim took it and went under it. Haynes went back. He landed against his horse and the beast held him. Jim said, 'Come in for more, you hoeman! Come in, plow pusher!'

Haynes was solid. Before it was over Jim knew he had been in a fight. He was standing only because he was about ten years younger than Haynes. But he had knocked the farmer cold.

'Anybody else feeling tough?'

A man said, 'You've got friends in this crowd, Jim.'

Clearness returned to the banker. 'Thanks for saying that, Leonard.' He blew his nose and spat. 'Get him off the street. He might attract flies, even though flies don't travel at night.'

Two men got Haynes on his feet, although his knees were rubber. They moved away toward the hotel with the farmer lurching and sagging between them. Jim went back into Doc Smith's office.

'Did you take him?' the medico asked.

Jim said, 'I guess so. I was on my boots. He wasn't.' His face didn't feel too good. Haynes had had a fist as big as an anvil and just as heavy. Or so it seemed to Jim. His lips, though, were not cut. Usually in a fight the first thing that happened was a cut lip that became very swollen. He glanced at himself in the mirror. He didn't look as bad as he felt, he decided. That first blow Haynes had got in—that sneaking, hard blow—had done the most damage. He saw something else in the mirror. Linda James was just entering the room.

'May I help you, Doctor Smith?'

Doc Smith turned and said, 'You sure can, Linda.' He was almost sober. His face was bloated and ugly and drink oozed out of his big pores. He looked at his fingers. 'Almost steady.'

Jim asked, 'You have to cut?'

'It's bedded down in him.'

Jake Stone opened his eyes. 'Cut away, sawbones. Get your meatsaw and go to work.' He looked at Linda. 'He runs around with a farmer girl and a cowman's daughter, and the gold is under his boots and he can't see it.' Only Linda heard that, and she blushed a little. Jim saw the blush but he did not know what caused it. She looked very pretty when she blushed. That thought was out of place when viewed against the tragedy and seriousness of the present situation.

'Can I help you, Doc?' he asked.

'Sure you can. By getting out of here.'

Jim looked at Linda James. 'I'll help the doctor.'

He went outside, and he was still sick at the core of his belly. Dan Shepard came up and asked, 'What happened?' Shepard was sleek and mysterious, and his presence was a rasp working on the edges of Jim's temper.

Jim said, 'Get the blazes out of here. We don't need you or your class, fellow. This was a good range until you moved in.'

'I'm giving you a run, eh?' Cynical.

Jim said, 'I can give you a better one,' and he moved ahead with doubled fists. Shepard went into a crouch with his fists up. Lamplight came through the window and showed on the sleek hard planes of his bronzed face. It glistened from eyes that no longer were tired-looking and sad. The man's jaw and lips were set and he was suddenly sleek and tough as a tiger. Jim got this impression and knew that Dan Shepard was a tough man. He had long suspected this. Now he knew for sure. Shepard had a goal here and he considered it a great goal. He would fight—yes, and maybe die—for his goal.

'Come ahead, banker.'

But before Jim could hit Deputy Will Lawson moved in and put his weight between them. He was a rock shoved ahead, solid and hard and strong; he put himself on wide thick legs.

'No more fights, Jim.'

Two townsmen moved in, and Jim felt a little touch of relief. Not that he was afraid of Dan Shepard—no, not that—but when he moved against Shepard he wanted to hit him once and only once. He wanted to settle it and forget it, and this was not the time or the place.

Shepard said, 'Some other time, Clayton.'

'Some other time.'

Lawson said, 'You an' me for your ranch, Jim.'

Jim went to the barn to get his bronc. The tension had run out of him, but the grains of it grated against him with the dull grind of sand. Dan Shepard said, 'Let me go, men,' and the townsmen dropped their hands from him. Shepard stood with his legs wide, and the lamplight showed his face clearly. There was raw red hell there, and the mask was gone; his emotions and hate lay stripped and bare, glistening with the metallic gleam of copper in a sun-washed rocky ledge. Those who watched saw this and were without words before it. The hate was there, and then it left before the push of reality, for at heart this man was a realist. Once he had been a romanticist, but Time had killed Fantasy; he was real now and he faced life with hard eyes. He heard the hoofs leave, heard them run out; only then did he turn and go to his office. He did not light a lamp. He walked in the dark, and Muggins ran scampering before him. He said, 'Damn you, cat, run!' Muggins brought to mind the memory of Ike Wilson. Shepard sat in the dark. His boots were out ahead of him as he slumped in his swivel chair. He waited.

An hour went by.

Still Dan Shepard waited. The excitement had left the main stem and a dog barked in the lonesome way that a dog barks at night. Another hour went by, and Shepard was silent. Then Ike Wilson came. He came silently, and the door opened with only a faint creak of hinges. Shepard's eyes were now used to the dark and he made out the form of his gunman.

'Ike.'

Ike Wilson had his hand on his gun. 'You, Dan?'

'Who the hell else would it be?'

'A man has to play his cards close in this game. He has to copper each an' every bet.'

'Sit down.'

Shepard heard the chair creak. Wilson moved in the chair, and Shepard heard the gentle sounds of leather rustling as the man's gun-harness moved. There was another sound then: a crackling sound.

'What is that sound?'

Wilson said, 'Muggins. Purrin'. Rubbin'

against my leg.'

'Kick him out.'

'No.' Wilson was stubborn. 'He's my friend.'

Shepard said, 'Talk, fellow.'

Ike Wilson had shot Jake Stone. Then he had burned down Jim Clayton's Bar T outfit.

'Burned it all, lock, stock an' barrel. Burned it plumb to the ground. Stone came close to pluggin' me. Bullets sang close. So he got to town, eh? How is he?'

'Don't know for sure. But I see Doc Smith's office is dark. So Jake Stone must be up at the hotel.'

'What's next?'

Shepard looked at his boots and found their faint outlines. 'They think for sure you were Hal Davis, man. I heard more than one may say that Davis had sneaked back to burn Clayton's outfit. Even that dumb deputy said that. From what I gather, Stone saw your outline but didn't recognize you. He said the man who shot him was built along the lines of Davis.'

'That's good.'

'Wonder where Davis is?'

Wilson asked, 'Ain't he contacted you yet?'

'If he had, would I have asked about him?'

'That's right.'

'Use your bean, Ike.'

'Don't rub me, fella.'

Shepard had no answer. He realized he had been a little too hasty. While Ike Wilson was ignorant—yes, almost stupid—he could still carry out orders, and he was a dangerous man because of his love for a dollar. He listened to Muggins purring. He hated the cat. He hated Wilson.

'Where is Clayton now, Dan?'

Shepard told his man that the banker and Deputy Will Lawson had headed out for the Bar T spread. This brought a chuckle from Wilson, who said, 'They can roast spuds in them ashes; some of them should still be hot. When I was a kid I used to swipe spuds—dig 'em up—an' roast them. Always tasted better'n those my ol' mother used to make, because mine was stoled.'

Shepard let the man ramble on.

Dan Shepard had his thoughts.

He remembered Jim Clayton challenging him. He remembered the shortness of Clayton's words. He remembered the way the banker had risen to meet the challenge. And he knew now—knew for sure—it was either Clayton or one Dan Shepard. So his job was to get Clayton killed.

'Ike?'

'Yeah.'

'Kill Clayton. Kill him as soon as you can.

Trail him and kill him. There's five hundred in it.'

'Five hundred?'

'Five hundred.'

Ike Wilson stood up. He took a step and kicked Muggins by accident, and the cat mewed and jumped. Wilson said sincerely, 'Sorry, my pal. I didn't see you.' Then to Dan Shepard, 'I'll think it over.'

Wilson went to the door. He had taken off his spurs, and therefore there was no noise of rowels as he walked on his toes. He put one hand on the knob, and then he said, 'It won't take no thinkin' over. When?'

'As soon as you can.'

'All right.'

Wilson closed the door and Dan Shepard listened for the sounds of the gunman moving away, but he received none. But this was idle and his thoughts were not idle long. He sat there and thought. Wilson was sure, and when Wilson acted he would act promptly and with great gunsmoke efficiency.

He would have to make sure that, at the time Jim Clayton was killed he, Dan Shepard, would be in the clear. This argument he had had with Clayton had not been good. The people in this town had heard them and had seen them go to the very verge of fistic argument. Therefore when Jim Clayton got killed they would instantly suspect him unless he were seen in some public place at the precise moment of Clayton's murder. Ike Wilson would undoubtedly be beyond suspicion. For Wilson was a farmer—or at least he was a farmer in the eyes of the local people—and Wilson had not made a dire threat against the person of Jim Clayton.

Shepard dozed.

When he awakened dawn was moving on mystic tiptoes across this range. Dawn was bending to kiss the sagebrush and greasewood, and the coming of dawn moved the buffalo grass and lifted dust slightly. Dawn touched the mountains with its fingertips, and glaciers and pines and lodgepoles returned the gesture. The Sioux moved from tepees along the Yellowstone, and a squaw grunted under her load of wood as her buck walked empty-handed. A buffalo bull pawed and snorted and dug and wondered what had become of his cows. And in Chicago, a man went to work, carrying his lunch pail. He hated his job. He hated the stink of steel. He would have loved the Montana dawn. But he was in Chicago and not in Montana.

CHAPTER FIFTEEN

Dawn also found Deputy Will Lawson and banker Jim Clayton looking at the ashes of Jim's Bar T outfit. And if the beauties of the Montana sunrise had any effect on Jim he did not show it. He stirred ashes idly with the toe of his boot. Whoever had burned down his outfit had done a good job. The log house was to the ground; the corrals had even been torched; the barn was ashes. The only building left standing was the outhouse. And one side of the privy was scorched from the flames of the barn.

'Done a right smart job,' the deputy grunted.

Jim had merely a nod.

The deputy said, 'Well, it's light enough to look for sign.' He moved out, bending his head toward the soil so that he looked like a squat English bulldog. Jim went into the brush. The dawn was not bright enough. He put his back to a cottonwood tree and waited for the light to come.

They had hit him twice; both blows had been strong. First they had robbed his bank and then they had burned his ranch to the sod. And who were *they*? He wished he knew for sure. He suspected Hal Davis of shooting Jake Stone. Davis had come back, and Davis had wanted some measure of revenge, and he had decided to burn down the Bar T. Davis had clashed with Jake Stone and had shot Jake.

Both blows had hit him hard. He had had almost every cent he owned invested in his ranch and the bank. Now his buildings were gone and his bank was deep in debt. At the rate he was going Dan Shepard would win.

That thought stirred him and was not pleasant. He could hear Lawson breaking brush; then these sounds soon died as the man went over a far ridge. Daylight was stronger, and Jim moved out to look for sign. He heard the brush crackle behind him and he knew the crackle was not made by Lawson, for Lawson was too far away. He turned.

Hal Davis had a Winchester .30–30, and the heavyset farmer wore a twisted smile on his whiskery face. He had the rifle up a little. One movement would level it; his forefinger would bend; the hammer would drop. Jim looked at the rifle and saw this and was careful.

'Be good,' Davis said quietly.

'You came back to the scene of your crime, eh?'

'Scene of my crime?' Was the surprised note in the farmer's voice genuine or was it feigned? 'I don't follow you, Clayton.'

'You sure you don't?'

'Don't talk in riddles. I ain't got much time. Thet deputy is scoutin' across the ridge. How did you two know I was in this territory? An' who burned down your outerfit? I came in on it about two hours ago an' it was still smokin'.'

Jim studied the man. Davis seemed to be telling the truth. 'You didn't know that Jake Stone got shot out here last night?'

'No, I didn't. Who shot him?'

'We all figure you shot him.'

Davis said, 'Another black mark against me, huh?' He spat, but his eyes were on Jim. 'Clayton, I hate your dirty face. I've had no use for you from the moment we tangled in that canyon when you stampeded my team. But this has gone far enough, man.'

'What do you mean?'

'I never robbed your bank. With God as my high witness, I repeat that statement: I did not rob your bank. Also before God I say I never fired your spread nor did I shoot your hired hand.'

'Before God, you say that?'

'Yes, before my Maker, sir.'

'There can be no higher oath than that,' Jim said. He watched the Winchester lower. 'Talk, Davis.'

Again Davis repeated that he had not robbed the Valley Center Bank. He said he had no knowledge of how to open locks. Jim reminded him that he had broken out of jail by using the handle of a spoon as a key. Davis smiled at this and said he had not opened the cell.

'I was in the same cell with a gent,' he said, 'and he was the one who opened the cell, not me. They caught him an' he laid the blame on me. Why, man, I can hardly open a bottle of beer without help.'

Jim nodded.

'Didn't the gink who rode over from the county seat tell you about the gent who broke jail with me?'

'No, he didn't.'

'Well, he did break me out.'

This conversation was leading nowhere, Jim figured. So he asked, 'Why are you talking to me? Why did you look me up? I'm your enemy. You admit that.'

'I think you are honest.'

'Thanks.' Dryly.

'I wanted to tell you I did not rob your bank. That money found on my farm was planted there.'

'Who planted it?'

Davis rested the butt of his rifle on the ground and looked at the barrel and showed deep thought. 'I've done a lot of thinkin' the few days I been in the clink. That's all I had to do.' He smiled a little at this statement. 'The evidence against me was all circumstantial, but they've hung men on circumstantial evidence. So I went over every man in this valley, one by one, and now I've settled on one.'

'Who is he?'

'You keep it to yourself if I tell you?'

'That I shall.'

'Ike Wilson.'

'Why Wilson?'

'Mrs. Carter was over to the county seat, and she came and visited me. She told me that she seen Wilson ride into town right after that holdup. He seemed kinda sneaky, she said; he went into Shepard's office by the back door, too.'

'Ride in *after* the holdup?'

'That means he was out of town for a spell. She'd seen him about midnight, she said; her youngest one was sick and she had to get Doc Smith up and she had seen Wilson in town. That was afore the bank got robbed.'

'Circumstantial.'

'Circumstantial put me behind bars. I've done thought over about Shepard, too. Maybe he ain't the angel some of these dumb farmers think he is. He's got a purpose. From what little I could hear in the sheriff's office, the railroad is not comin' through Valley Center.

It's anglin' toward Lewistown, the Law said. That means us farmers are left holdin' the sack. Who put us there?' He answered his own question. 'Dan Shepard. An' who is Dan's righthand man?' He answered that, too. 'None other than one Ike Wilson.'

'I'll get the Law to look up Wilson's past.' Jim glanced to where Deputy Will Lawson had gone over the ridge. 'What are you going to do, Davis?'

Davis was going to take it on the dodge and try to pin this trouble onto somebody. Jim warned him to stay away from Belle and his mother, for the Law was watching the Davis farm. Davis smiled and said he knew that much; he had that much brains. When he got cleared of this he was pulling out of Valley Center for good. But not until he was cleared. He was stubborn and proud, and Jim liked these traits in the man. He found himself believing the farmer. Davis had made his pledge before his Redeemer, and Jim had heard that the man was religious. Therefore the oath was good and the oath was strong.

'Stay around close to this place,' Jim said. 'If I need you I'll hang a white shirt on the clothes line.'

The clothes line was still standing. One end of it was tied to the privy and the other end was anchored to a post that had not burned.

'All right, Clayton.'

'Better make it back into the brush,' Jim warned. 'That deputy should be coming back soon.'

Jim was standing by what *had been* his barn when Deputy Lawson returned. He had hit the signs of a shod horse and he had followed them to the wagon road and then lost them.

'Danged farmers and their rigs had tromped up the road so much that a man cain't foller sign in the dust ... so I lost the tracks. You find anythin', Mr. Clayton?'

'Not a sign.'

'Work thet country good?'

'Sure did. Every inch of it.'

Lawson swung up and caught his reins. 'No percentage in stickin' aroun' here. Whoever did it made good his get-a-way an' left danged little sign, an' I ain't no nose-dog to smell him out.' He sighed. 'Well, that's the way law work is—slow an' roun' an' roun'—an' you figure you're gettin' nowhere in a hell of a rush and then—boom!—just like that the case pops an' is settled. Sometimes it is settled in gun-smoke. Like the time over on the Poplar River...'

Jim listened, nodded, had his thoughts. They came into town and went down and ate in the café. Jim left the deputy and looked in on his bank. His bookkeeper was on the job, the place was confining, and he stayed only a short time. He knocked on Mrs. Carter's door, and she said, 'Well, bless my buttons, but it is Jim Clayton! Jim, have you et?'

He had *et*, and he thanked the matron. Her husband was handy man in the Mercantile and was at work. Kids were all over the house. They gawked at him. One was in diapers. Jim said, 'Wasn't he sick a while back?'

He had been. The night he had been ill the bank had been robbed. Jim tried to make his questions discreet and subtle, but it was difficult. One kid jumped on his shoulders and made a race horse out of him. His mother unceremoniously jerked the young jockey from the saddle. She batted him in the back of his lap and he went off bawling. The one in diapers bawled in sympathy. They made quite a lot of noise. Mrs. Carter brushed a stray wisp of hair back.

'Sometimes I think my husband and me have made lots of mistakes. Yes, I met Ike Wilson on the street. Yes, I saw him ride into town. Say, who have you been talkin' with to tell you this?'

'Doc Smith mentioned to me he had got out of bed to treat your young one. I came over just as a good neighbor, Mrs. Carter, to see how he was.'

'You father used to visit us, too. He was a

wonderful man, Jim, and you're gettin' more like your good father every day.'

'Thank you.' Jim essayed modesty. He wanted to get out of here. He had found out nothing substantial. He finally made his escape, and out on the street he found dust and heat and silence. When he was in front of the Town Hotel he saw that Linda James sat on the bench in the shade. He dropped into place beside her and they sat for a few moments in silence after they had exchanged greetings.

She said, 'Your buildings?'

'A total loss.' He did not mention that the privy still stood.

'Any clues?'

'None.'

She looked out into the street. He saw her profile. 'Your girl friend is in town?'

'Which one?'

'The Davis girl.'

'Oh, that's nice.'

'Who did you suspect I meant?'

'Maybe Cynthia Nelson,' he said.

'Quite a girl. She'll make somebody a good wife. So will Miss Davis. The home-loving type. Lots of children.'

Jim almost shuddered, remembering the Carter household.

'What's the matter?'

'Two is enough,' Jim said.

She smiled, and he liked her smile. 'I saw you go over to Mrs. Carter's. I'm just needling you, if you don't know it.' Her smile left and she was very sober. 'Jim, I have something I should tell you.'

'Yes?'

The man he had whipped—Haynes—had spent the forenoon in the Silver Dollar engaging in a bout with John Barleycorn, and John was ahead on points. He hadn't floored Haynes in a physical contest, but he had downed him mentally. Haynes was claiming he would kill one Jim Clayton.

'You beat him up pretty badly.'

'He did his share to me.'

'You don't look bad.'

Jim got to his feet and thanked her. He saw Dan Shepard come out of his office. The land-locator stood in the shade and looked across the street. His glance met Jim's and then went on. Shepard returned to his den.

Jim went in to see Elmer Hawkins first. Hawkins was sitting in his chair and grumbling against the heat, his wound, and old Doc Smith. Jim then went to see Jake Stone. Mrs. Runden was nursing Jake, and the foreman was pretty weak. Doc Smith claimed he would pull through, the woman said, and Jake confirmed this opinion. The

Bar T foreman joked a little, but he was very sick, Jim noticed. Jim left with a tight feeling down in his belly right under his belt buckle. He'd like to meet the gent that shot Jake.

He went to his bank. It was cooler in the thick-walled building. His bookkeeper nodded, and Jim went back to his office and sat down. It seemed as though the walls moved in and confined him. He realized then he would rebuild his Bar T buildings. He was primarily an outdoor man. He remembered how Linda James' eyes had sparkled when she had talked about a ranch. A woman and a man could raise good kids and lots of kids if they made them mind. Now why had he thought of that? He blamed the thought on his visit to the Carter home. Carter never paid much attention to his kids, and his wife was too harried and pressed to discipline them.

His meeting with Hal Davis was brought to mind. He felt sure the farmer was innocent. The whole thing pivoted around Dan Shepard. But what could he prove? One word answered that question, and the word was *Nothing*. Shepard had come out of his office and looked up and down and across the street, and the last person his gaze had shifted to had been himself, Jim Clayton. Jim knew now he was marked. Haynes had made a boast and Shepard could use this. Hal Davis had made the same error that Haynes had made. Davis had made his boast, too, against him and it had boomeranged against the farmer and put him behind the bars. Now Hal Davis was a hunted outlaw. There was irony in that and it was grim. The first day Jim had met Davis the farmer had been just a simple farmer. Now he was an outlaw wanted for bank robbery, for wounding an officer of the law, and for a jail delivery. Yes, and Deputy Lawson also claimed that Davis had burned down the Bar T. Well, that assumption was logical, Jim realized.

Who would move against him first? Would it be Ike Wilson, or would the opponent be none other than Dan Shepard? Jim thought, It's time I get a hand in this game, and it's time I do some brain work. He got his idea by simmering this down to its bare rib-like structure. So far the hitting had come in the night and in the brush. He would find the right spot and the right time and keep alert. He went over his trap and found it logical. Some parts of it, of course, rested on coincidence. Or call it fate, for want of a fitting name.

But he wanted wider borders, so he went outside again. He got a fresh bronc and left town and wondered if he were being trailed. Haynes had made his boast and Haynes would follow through. And if Haynes did not hit then another party would to make it look as though it were Haynes' work. Of this he was certain.

He stopped among rocks that hid him. He climbed mesas and watched with his field glasses. He hid in high brush and watched his back-trail and yet he saw no rider or riders on it. He watched with great patience, for his life now depended upon patience. If they put him away for good then there would only be Old Hans Nelson to get rid of. And Old Hans was an old man whose power was spent and who now talked to bolster what pride remained in his scraggly carcass. Still he saw no trailers. This was a game of hide and seek. Only this was not play—this was real—and in the core of its reality lay a grim danger. He was sure he was being trailed. With Haynes' boast fresh in the minds of the Valley Center people his opponent—or opponents—would be sure to strike.

They had to strike.

Dusk came, and still he saw nobody. He talked with Deputy Will Lawson, and they sat their broncs at the base of Shadow Butte. Shadows moved and blended, caused by the dry wind in the pines silhouetted against the sky; Jim caught the smell of pine tar and pitch. A cottontail rabbit hopped out of the brush about fifty yards away. He nibbled on green grass that grew along the base of a pine. Snow water had been held at this point later in the season because of the shade of the pine, and therefore there was a bit of green grass.

Lawson said, 'A peaceful animal, and all hands are against him. Man creates his trouble through greed and earns his trouble, but a rabbit gets his through misfortune and accident of birth.'

'No luck, Will?'

Lawson sighed. 'No luck... Where do you ride, friend?'

'My outfit.'

'Only ashes.'

Jim nodded.

Lawson said, 'Haynes made his boast.'

'Haynes,' Jim said, 'is full of hot air. I could say he is full of somethin' else, but I'll be polite.'

'A bullet ain't perlite.'

'Neither am I.' Jim smiled.

Once he glanced back, and he saw that the deputy sat his saddle and watched him. He was solid, this man Lawson. He was an oak and he had his legs into the soil; the soil seemed to give him strength. Jim wondered, Will he follow me? And when he got to the lift of the ridge he looked back. Lawson still sat his bronc at the same spot. The hill rose and hid the man, and Jim rode on. He stood on his stirrups and fell into the rhythm of his horse's progress. He crossed a mountain park where once grass had stood high and had moved in the wind and rippled against space. But now the grass was short and brown and lazy. The drouth had killed its growth. The roots of course were still there, for the root of grass is tougher than the blades, its by-product. He met another rise and he glanced back. He saw Lawson then, and the man was a black ant against space as he labored across the dusty plain. Jim thought, He's going toward town, and he looked again for a pursuer but saw no sign. He turned his glasses on the higher lifts and still saw nothing, and he frowned and thought, Maybe my plan is wrong. But deep inside he doubted this conjecture.

His cattle were gaunt. On Rimrock Ridge he met Old Hans. The old viking was hot; he slouched in his old saddle. Cattle were poor. The sun would raise more hell. Blast this hot wind. Blast the nesters. He'd run them out, he would; no, let the drouth do it. No, he'd run them out, he would.

'Cyn leaves us, Jim.'
'When?'
'Tomorrow.'
Old eyes searched Jim's face.
'I'll miss her, Old Hans.'

The eyes probed. They were invisible hands feeling him to find the contour of his thoughts. They failed.

'The young,' said the old cowman, 'have to leave the home sometime. We parents are selfish. Blow, damn you, blow—you dry wind.' He looked back at Jim. 'Where do you ride for, son?'

Jim told him.

'Haynes talked in town. You hit a dangerous man. I've seen his face. You look rough, but he looks beat up. Watch your hoof tracks, son; the ones that run behind you. Keep watching.'

'You think Haynes is dangerous?'

'I do.'

'He's being used,' Jim said. 'They're all being used, those farmers. They might wake up. Some have opened their eyes, I think.'

'There's Hal Davis too, Jim.'

Jim smiled. 'They're on all sides of me.' That was correct, too. There was Davis, and he had sworn on his God; still, Davis was dangerous. Or was he dangerous? Jim remembered the broken, simple light in the man's eyes. He had a hunch that if and when Davis were cleared of the charges against him, Hal Davis would move away from this basin. He was the type who wanted no trouble. Jim saw that now. But there was in Hal Davis a tough unbending pride that demanded he clear his name before he move on to some new spot. Davis had the same as told this to him, even though the disclosure had come through hinting only. Jim remembered Belle Davis. She had the form, she had the character; once she had stirred him—now that feeling was gone. Where had it gone to? Why had he lost it?

'So long, son.'

He watched the patriarch lope across the park. He sat his saddle and he was a part of his bronc, for the saddle was a part of him. His years and his life had demanded this. The wind had been his against his face, he had seen cattle string out and plunge into the rolling waters of the Arkansas; he had made medicine with the Cheyennes and the Sioux. But progress—if such it could be called—had almost beaten him. For he had refused to synchronize his thinking to a new era. Jim thought, Good old man, and he wondered again if he would miss Cynthia. Of course he would miss her. He had known her all his life. Her brother Joe had been his good friend. Old Hans would miss her and Mrs. Nelson would miss her daughter.

Jim turned his horse.

He looked at more of his cattle. Gradually the drouth, coupled with a shortage of water and of grass, was dragging flesh off his stock. The wolves were making some inroads but not causing too much of a loss. He hated the big, shaggy loafer wolves. They were big and rough and they hit without warning, and somehow they reminded him of Dan Shepard, even though Shepard was smooth and subtle. He remembered the look on Shepard's face when he had challenged the land-locator. For in that moment anger and its heat had melted the subtle cover of civilization from the man's face and had left him strong and ruthless. The mask had been ripped off and Shepard had shown his true nature.

And always he watched his back-trail. And he saw nothing out of place. Heat hung across the basin. It clung to the dusty soil and tasted eagerly of whatever little bits of greenery were left. Wheat scorched even further and heads would not form. Oats dropped on stems and fell to the ground. Grasshoppers buzzed. What the lack of rain did not kill the grasshoppers finished. There had been very few hoppers until the farmers had come in. Some claimed hopper eggs had come in with seed wheat. Jim didn't know; he didn't care. The hoppers were here and that was that. They buzzed and rose ahead of him. They reached the higher air and circled and buzzed still more. He hated them.

Dusk found him riding into what had been the yard of the Bar T. The burned down buildings seemed to mock him. He felt suddenly desperate. He had the feeling of a man who is fleeing and who is being pressed hard by his pursuers, and who suddenly comes to a wild raging river he cannot swim. There are no trees to climb. Only instead of running, Jim was chasing: or was he the pursuer? Yes, in a way—for he was setting a trap.

Would it work?

Would the killer—or killers—come?

He thought, Time'll tell. He did not think of Cyn or Belle, and when a young man does not entertain the thought of a young woman in the back of his head then he is indeed busy with other thoughts.

He hid his bronc under a ledge that was already growing dark with shadows. The heat rolled off the earth, wave after wave; the earth rose and swelled in the heat; gradually the night hid its rise. But the coming of night did not quench the heat, for the land had no water to cool it. At midnight it would still be very hot. Down in town, in the farmhouses, at the Circle S, men and women would lie in bed, letting the bedclothes lie in a pile; they would roll in the heat. Gradually sleep would come, but not because the land cooled. Sleep would come because of great fatigue. This land had no water to cool it.

He waited. Time moved on. Darkness grew, broke slightly, gathered again. Once he thought he heard a noise. He was not sure. The cougar and coyote and wolf are sleek and fleet and silent. Dawn broke the sky, and then the man came. And he came to kill Jim Clayton.

Jim was sure of that.

CHAPTER SIXTEEN

This man died sitting with his back against the rough bark of a pine tree that had seen buffalo and redskins move across the park it faced. He died with his back against the tree and with two of Jim Clayton's bullets in him. The first had hit him in the chest, high on the right side; the second had broken a hole in his belly. Now he sat with his back against this tree and he was ready to die. He knew he was going to die. He leaned his head back and closed his eyes, and Jim stood and watched. Jim felt very bad. He hated to have to kill this man. But the man had shot at him; the man had tried his level best to kill him. He should have hated the man, but he did not hate him; rather, he felt sorry for him. Sorry because the man had allowed hate and greed to boss him, to dominate him.

Jim said, 'You tried to murder me. I shot only to defend my person. It was either you or me.'

'I made my play.'

'Why?'

'I hate you. I hate your guts.'

Jim said, 'There was this money in your pocket. When I moved you here it fell free and I picked it up. Did somebody pay you to murder me?'

No answer.

'I asked a question.'

'I'll be soon where you can ask and be damned. Have you got the makin's, banker?'

Jim rolled a cigaret. He lit it and put it in the man's mouth. The man puffed and then coughed and the cigaret fell.

'My lungs are shot.'

Jim nodded.

There was a silence. Then the mocking noise of a bluejay broke it. He **was saucy** and noisy and he didn't know **a man was dying.** And had he known that simple fact he undoubtedly would have kept on talking anyway.

'Somebody pay you?' Jim asked.

'Yes.'

'Who was it?'

'Find that out for yourself, banker.'

Jim stood and looked down. There was nothing he could do. While the man had been unconscious he had ripped off the fellow's shirt and bound the torn strips around his chest. The makeshift bandage was red now, and blood oozed from the hole in the man's side. Blood made a round, bubble-like ring against the clean whiteness of his flesh. Jim figured the wound was bleeding inside. He knew this was the dangerous wound; this would kill the man.

He wished the fellow would talk. He did not want to see the man die without telling him who had hired him to ride out to kill. He looked down on the wounded man and had his thoughts. The fellow sat with his back to the tree, and his back was bowed and his head lopped on his chest. Only his hands seemed alive. They rested on the sod, and occasionally they clenched into the earth as pain rode its roughshod way through his body. They clenched and unclenched and unconsciously they lifted and pulled at the soil which soon would claim them and this man's body. Jim had this thought and felt very sick. He wondered whether Death was a tragedy or a blessing. Some day he would find the answer, as all living things must some day find the answer. This man was close to solving the Eternal Riddle. Jim tried to make himself tough and angry and glad that he had shot this man. But for some reason the toughness and the anger would not come.

He and this gent had played a rough and tough game of .30–30 pool. They had used .30–30 rifles for cues and .30–30 bullets for pool balls. They had made quite a few shots within the fierce few moments that the battle had run its course. But he had put the most balls in the pockets.

The man had trailed him, although never once—until the firing had started—had Jim glimpsed him. This man was a terrier on the trail; he could move from brush to brush; even a Sioux buck would not have seen him. He had made one—and only one—error. This error had cost him his life. He had not wormed his way close enough before taking his first shot. He had shot from the rimrock, and the distance had been too far for accurate Winchester work. The bullet had come close, but closeness did not count; only direct hits counted. Then the work had started—tough and deadly rifle work. You wormed your way through the brush and you came to a clearing. Dart across that clearing, fellow, and get killed—then you'll be in the open. Work over this way, Jim Clayton. Now stop, Jim, and hide in those boulders; think this over, Jim, and figure out your opponent's next move. Brains has a part in this; bullets won't win it all.

So with this combination—with brains and bullets—Jim had made his play. And he had caught this man running across a clearing. Now bring up your Winchester, Jim; let those sights fall into line—get them lined up quickly, Jim; now let that hammer fall—there, you got him. He stumbled and he's falling, but now he's on one knee and his rifle is coming up. Jack down on that lever, Jim Clayton; listen to that new cartridge slide into the barrel, listen to the metallic click as the barrel is loaded; look—his shot missed. He's wild and sick, and shoot him again even though your belly is revolting. Now he's down. You've won, Jim, you've won! What's the matter, Jim? You don't feel like shouting in joy? Why, he aimed to kill you, didn't he? Had he killed you he'd have been shouting now and you would have been dead...

'Why don't you talk to me?' Jim's voice was kindly. 'I think you'll feel better, sir.'

The man tried to laugh. Maybe you could call it a laugh, but it was silent even though his mouth did open. After a while he said, 'Why should I take anybody else into this? I'll be over the Ridge soon, Clayton. You can't get a word out of me. Oh, yes, you can: I robbed your bank. There's somebody comin' through the brush, ain't they?'

Hal Davis came out of the buckbrush. He carried his rifle. 'I heard shots,' he said. 'I was camped on the rimrock.' He looked at the wounded man. 'Nobody else but Ike Wilson, eh?'

Jim said, 'It was me or him.'

'Dan Shepard,' Davis said. 'He's behind this. What has he told you, Jim?'

'He admits he robbed the bank.'

'Then that clears me.' Davis spoke to Wilson, who watched him with sunken, sick eyes. 'You stole my bronc, eh? You planted that dinero on my property?'

'How did you guess it?' Wilson was cynical.

Davis said, 'I'd liked to have matched rifles with you, Wilson.'

'You'll never get the chance.'

Wilson's head went down. He seemed to be sleeping. He was sick and he was tired, and he looked like a sleepy boy. The sunlight glistened on the waves of his dark hair. He had run his race and his whip had been the greedy cutting whip of greed. Now he slept and greed was forgotten. Jim and Davis looked at him and then at each other. Jim said, 'I wish he'd get evidence against Shepard.'

'He won't.'

Jim shook his head. 'He won't talk against Shepard.'

'You don't need that evidence. He's told you where the dinero is buried. That saves your bank. And I figure all you think about is money.'

'You're bitter, Davis.'

'You need no evidence against Shepard. The very fact that this man came to kill you—and the evidence of this money this gent toted in his pocket—shows somebody hired him to kill you. And who would it be but Dan Shepard?'

'You need evidence to stand up in court.'

Davis laughed harshly. 'You blamed fool, Clayton, this will never get to anybody's court but the court of ol' man Colt. Shepard will make his move and make it fast, and it won't be with the Law behind him.'

Wilson said, 'He's right, banker.'

Jim quickly seized his opportunity. 'Then you admit that Shepard hired you to kill me?'

'Don't jump to wild ideas. I admit nothin'. I'm branchin' off the trail at this point. You ride that way and I ride this way. I don't give a tinker's damn what happens to you. You figure out your own ideas, banker. The only reason I told you where this money is hid—the only reason I told you that I robbed the bank—'

Wilson stopped.

Jim waited.

Davis waited.

Davis said, 'That crazy bluejay is nuts.'

Wilson said, 'I tol' you that because of Belle.'

'Belle?' Davis asked.

Wilson said, 'A man makes a move and he's beyond the pale. Then a good woman won't look at him. He lives his secret life and he has his secret thoughts. I told you that because of her.'

Davis said, 'Thanks, Ike.'

'Anything else?' Jim asked.

Silence again. Then the bluejay's screams. These died and silence came on. Ike Wilson did not raise his head. His voice was a rambling monotone, and his words were not clear because they did not separate themselves properly.

'Man is a nutty duck. He fights for little things an' he lets the big things go by. I'm as crazy as the rest. Yep, one thing, Clayton.'

'And that?'

'Muggins.'

Jim looked at Davis and frowned in puzzlement. Then he looked back at the man who sat with his back against the tree and with his head down.

'The tomcat?' Jim asked.

'Yes, the tomcat.'

Jim said, 'He won't trust me. He hates everybody but you. I've tried to pet him and he's run away. But I'll feed him for you.'

'Set his food in the alley. He'll eat if nobody is around. I wish he was here. I'd like to have him rub against me an' purr. He did that the first day I met him. He hates Shepard.'

Davis said, 'That seems to be a common habit around here.'

'You'll do that for Muggins?'

Jim thought, He's dying, and he hired out to kill me, and yet he's worried about an old alley cat. He said, 'For you and for Muggins, Wilson.'

'Thanks, Jim.'

After a while they tied the dead man across his saddle. Davis said, 'I'll go into town with you, Jim,' and Jim nodded. They rode at a walk, and Jim led the horse that carried Ike Wilson's body. The horse smelled blood and associated this smell with death and he wanted to buck.

But Hal Davis put his quirt across the bronc's rump, and this took such ideas out of his hammerhead. Then Davis rode even with Jim and said, 'Another terrible day of heat. Feel it rolling acrost the plain? Inside of an hour it'll be an oven. Look. Dust is blowing already.'

'The plow loosened it.'

'I see that now. Well, it's me for out of this country, Clayton. With what Wilson told you, I'll be clear of the Law except for that jail delivery. But that won't mean much, seein' the bank robbery is solved, will it?'

'I'll see you through, Hal.'

'We both got off on the wrong foot, Jim. These other farmers are ready to move. When we leave the whole bunch will leave, I figure. This is a cow country an' nothin' else, an' not too good a cow country at that. Nothin' when you compare it with the Elkhorn region over in Nebrasky.'

'Shepard will make his play. He won't run.'

Davis nodded. 'You're right there, Jim. He's got ideas and designs and he wants this land. He won't run. What will you do?'

'I was here before Shepard.'

'Bull-headedness?'

Jim looked at the stocky farmer. 'No, not that. Shepard hired a man to try to kill me. I'm not fighting over a cow or a piece of land or a woman. I'm fighting to keep alive. If I don't kill him then he'll kill me. You see that, don't you?'

'Yes, you're right.'

The dawn had changed into forenoon. True to Hal Davis' prophecy, the heat was growing.

Again it would lift what little moisture the soil had; again it would suck at the leaves of trees for moisture. Their broncs plodded into the heat. Wilson's horse had settled down and was obedient on the end of the hackamore rope. Jim kept thinking of Valley Center town. Dan Shepard would be down there and Shepard would be waiting for Wilson.

Well, Shepard would soon meet Wilson.

And then there was also Jake Stone. Jake Stone had one of Wilson's bullets in him. Ike Wilson had admitted shooting at Jake. Shepard had paid him for that too. Wilson had not mentioned that Shepard had paid him. Ike Wilson had seemed to have a great respect for Dan Shepard, and he had said little or nothing to involve the land-locator in this trouble. Shepard had, in a distant way, been his friend. And he had remained true to that friendship until eternal sleep had closed his eyes forever.

But still, when you've known a man all your life, when he taught you how to sit your first saddle, he's a part of your life and you owe him much. And when he is shot defending your property, working for you—that is also a great proof of great friendship. And Jim kept remembering these things.

'Valley Center,' Davis murmured.

They rode into the alley behind the Silver Dollar. The girl known as Jeff was hanging up some stockings. She stretched to reach the clothesline, for she was short and small, and Jim saw her pretty knees. Only at this time he had little eye for them.

She saw them and said, 'Oh!'

Jim nodded, and Davis nodded.

She came to the alley. Her face was flushed. Her eyes went to Davis, then to Jim.

'That's Ike Wilson. He's dead?'

'I killed him,' Jim said.

'Oh.'

They rode on. She watched them. Davis said, 'She liked Ike. She's just a prostitute, but she has her likes, I guess. Odd that she'd care for clumsy, ugly Ike.'

Jim nodded.

A cat ran across the alley. He climbed a shed and then sat on the edge of the low roof. When Jim rode by he looked directly at the cat, who sat there at eye level and watched him. Tawny beast. Cat eyes. Fold your front paws under you and look at foolish men with wise eyes.

'Muggins,' Hal Davis said.

Jim said, 'Yep, Muggins.'

CHAPTER SEVENTEEN

It was the girl called Jeff who told Dan Shepard about the death of his man, Ike Wilson. Shepard was haggard, and his tie, for once, was askew. No longer was he immaculate and groomed. The night had been without sleep and filled with worry, and blue whiskers covered his jaws. He had spent the night in his office waiting for Ike Wilson. Hours had moved across space and still Wilson had not returned. He had thought of riding out into the night and looking for Wilson, and then he had discarded that plan. For one thing, the night was too dark to see very clearly. And for another, Wilson was tough and smart enough to kill a man. Then why had not Wilson returned? Shepard had a reason for this. Wilson had not got close enough to make a successful kill. He was biding his time. Dawn would bring him back. There was no use in riding out.

So Shepard had dozed in his swivel chair. He was, in fact, dozing when Jeff broke in. When he heard her open the door he reached for his rifle that stood beside his desk.

'What is it, Jeff?'

'Ike Wilson,' she said. 'He's dead.'

Shepard thought, So this is it, and he watched her. By will power he kept his face without emotion.

'Who killed him?'

She told about talking to Jim Clayton and Hal Davis. Shepard heard her words and watched her face and thought, This *sure* is it. He had long expected this, and in his mind he had prepared himself for this moment and its significance. Therefore he felt no shock. He was as calm as when he faced everyday life.

'You know, Dan, I sort of liked that big guy. He was stupid, sure, but there was something about him—something boyish—' She did not finish. She put her hands over her eyes and started to weep. Shepard watched her. She turned and ran out the back door and hurried up the alley.

Shepard got to his feet. He jacked the rifle open and looked at the ugly rim of the unfired cartridge that was in the barrel. He opened the front door and placed the rifle, butt down, on the sidewalk. The front sight rested against the frame building. He adjusted the rifle with great care and in the proper position. He thought his hands were steady. But he looked at them and saw they shook slightly.

He thought, I got to stop that.

He stood in his office and held his hands out, fingers wide and extended, and they still shook. He put power into his fingers and pulled them back and made a fist of his brown hand. Then slowly he re-extended his fingers, keeping the muscles taut; this time they were solid and had lost their trembling.

He thought, That's the way they should be.

Muggins came in the back door. Shepard turned quickly. When he saw the cat he kicked, but Muggins saw that the boot missed. The tomcat made his back into a question mark and hissed and his tail spread in anger. Then he walked out again, not hurrying, not running.

He's looking for Ike Wilson. Well, he'll never see Ike again.

Dan Shepard took his gun harness from the wooden peg driven into a stud on the wall. He put it around his slender waist, shrugged it into position, and then he meticulously tied down each holster. Run the buckskin thong under each thigh, Shepard, and now feel the grate of it against your fingers as you make your knot. Have the thong tight so that when you lift your gun the holster does not hang but stays close to your leg.

He tested the holsters by lifting his guns, and then he turned his attention to the Colts themselves. Break open the loading gates and see that the cylinders are loaded with their ugly messages and then turn the cylinders and make sure they click into place for accurate spacing. A man's life depends on small things. The lift of a leaf, the slow turn of the wind, the stirring of dust. Yes, and the rhythmic beat of his heart. A man moves in the night and rifles talk and that man is dead. He's jackknifed across a bronc up the street, and the man who killed him is waiting for you. That man will take the corpse to the morgue in the hardware store.

Shepard thought, I'm ready.

He reviewed things in his mind. He made a mental map of the street, the hardware store, the other buildings. Outside, men and women were hurrying toward the other end of the street. They went by his door and some glanced in as they passed, but nobody said a word to him. They were going up to see the corpse. Well, Ike, you have an audience, at long last. For once you have the center of the stage, Ike Wilson.

I'm ready.

He looked up the street. Yes, he was in front of the hardware store, standing beside the horse that carried Ike. One shot from the Winchester and you've killed Jim Clayton, he thought. But that would never work. There would be a cottonwood tree and a noose and that noose would do its work. Ambush did not pay. Ambush meant only death. The other was fifty-fifty.

A man said, 'Jim, Shepard is in his office. He's put his rifle out on the sidewalk, and if he needs it it is handy. When I went by he was lookin' at his guns.'

'Thanks, Webster.'

'Jim, Jake Stone died last night. Doc Smith told me he passed on about two o'clock—'

Jim looked at the man and did not see him. 'Thanks, Webster.'

'Jim, I'm sorry, fella.'

So Jake had died. Jake had ridden a rough saddle; the dust had swirled upward; the bronc had bucked. Ride 'im, Jake; ride 'im, friend! Kick him high ahead, Jake; scratch him behind. Jake, see that Circle S calf? Catch him for the iron, Jake. Listen to that catchrope cut the air. Best manila rope a man can buy. Sing, manila, sing! Lord, the things a man thinks of, the things he remembers.

But a man can only stand there and say, 'Thanks, Webster.'

Somebody said, 'Carry this stiff into the hardware store, men. Hanson, get his head; Parker, his feet. I'll take the middle. Shucks, he ain't heavy, is he? Lord, those bullets almost busted him in two.'

Hal Davis said, 'It ain't my fight, Clayton.'

'I know that.'

Davis said, 'Here comes Dan Shepard.'

Notice how the people scatter away from you, Jim? They're like sagehens running when a coyote shows his pointed snout. Some of them wish they had wings like a sagehen, too; then they could flee faster.

Jim moved away from his bronc. He watched Dan Shepard and he was very quiet. He remembered the big game with Idaho. Before you moved into the line you were jumpy and then, back down, rump down, you got silent and tough. Send the halfback over! Send him into my tackle position! That was the way he felt now. He was glad about that. Very glad.

'You hired a man to kill Jake Stone, Shepard.'

Shepard watched and made no answer.

'You hired a man to kill me. I killed him instead. I lay the murder of Jake Stone at your dirty boots. This will never get to a higher court.'

'This is high enough.'

Jim said, 'Pull, man!'

They were there, and the street was dusty and people watched. The halfback was coming over, cleats ground, interference formed. A sea of backs, and they smashed at his tackle slot. One of them hit him high on the right shoulder. The blow turned him, stunned him, but he watched and waited. His gun was roaring, talking, doing its work. He felt it in his fist. It seemed remote and distant, yet it kicked against his palm. He thought, I broke up that play.

A crazy thought...

But Dan Shepard was sitting in the dust. The seat of his expensive trousers was flat in the Montana dust. His Colt lay about ten feet away, spun out there by Jim's bullets. His right hand gun. He now tried to pull his other gun. His hand moved, Jim steadied; the hand fell down. Shepard put his knuckles into the dust. He looked at Jim, and his face was still hard.

'You win,' he said.

That was all. He died the way a man should die—proud, unbending, still hitting for his goal. And when Jim turned away he felt as though he too would like to die. His shoulder ached. But the ache was nothing compared to the ache in his heart.

He thought, Only Time will help me.

And then he saw her.

She stood on the edge of the plank sidewalk across the street. Fear had left her heart and she had color now. But when the guns had made their ugly noises she had had no color. She was small, she was feminine, and she was what a man desired. She had waited long for this time and this man. She had met men whom she could have won, and now she had met the right one and she had almost lost him.

Jim read this and he remembered little things, little words: I love the outside, and the dust, and I can see cattle moving down from the foothills, going down to water. I'm dark and small and yet I hold promise, Jim. There is gold under your feet, under your boots, and you cannot see it. Jim, you can't see the forest because of the trees.

He moved across the street.

He said, 'Come here.'

But she was already helping him. She said, 'Your arm is broken. I can tell by the way it dangles. Jim, oh, Jim.'

'Don't talk,' he said gently.

She took his hand and they walked toward the hotel. Jim looked at her and felt her warmth surround him and knew then of the days ahead. You come out of the forest, out of the dark, and you come to the tall grass of a mountain park. Then you turn and look back, and the sun is moving over the tip of the peak, and you have left the dark and come into the light. Behind you is the forest, dark and heavy and smelling of tar and pitch, with its lodgepoles rough under your hands, and you stand in the tall grass and the sun washes over you and the sun is clean and good.

'Linda,' he said, 'I love you.'

She said, 'Jim, I've loved you since the moment I first saw you.' And then she was laughing and weeping at the same time.

He put his good arm around her and held her. They stood there in the lobby of the hotel, and the old clerk watched and smiled the benevolent smile of a man who watches something he likes to see.

Photoset, printed and bound in Great Britain by
REDWOOD BURN LIMITED, Trowbridge, Wiltshire